The first touch ignited a flame that blew Holt's earlier conviction—that his fascination with her was a passing thing—wide apart, like a pallet of dynamite

He slanted his mouth over hers, taking nibbling bites from her plush lower rim, pulling it inside his mouth and lavishing it with his tongue. She whimpered when he released it, only to glide his tongue across the seam of her lips in a sensual seesawing motion until she parted her lips for him, silently inviting him inside.

When he felt her tentatively reach out and wrap her arms loosely around his neck, Holt brought her closer, flush against him, her soft curves molding against his hard body. Her big, beautiful breasts pressed tightly against his chest.

He was on fire for her. What had started out as a simple need to taste her, to find out if her lips were as soft as they looked, had escalated into a blazing need that was beginning to consume him.

And damned if he didn't want to get devoured in the blaze.

Books by Kimberly Kaye Terry

Kimani Romance

Hot to Touch
To Tempt a Wilde
To Love a Wilde

KIMBERLY KAYE TERRY

Kimberly Kaye Terry's love for reading romances began at an early age. Long into the night, she would stay up until she reached "The End" with her Mickey Mouse night-light on, praying she wouldn't be caught reading what her mother called "those" types of books. Often, she would acquire her stash of "those" books from beneath her mother's bed. Ahem. To date she's an award-winning author of fourteen novels in romance and erotic romance, has garnered acclaim for her work and happily calls writing her full-time job.

Kimberly has a bachelor's degree in social work and a master's in human relations and has held licenses in social work and mental health therapy in the United States and abroad. She volunteers weekly at various social-service agencies and is a long-standing member of Zeta Phi Beta Sorority, Inc., a community-conscious organization. Kimberly is a naturalist and practices aromatherapy. She believes in embracing the powerful woman within each of us and meditates on a regular basis. Kimberly would love to hear from you. Visit her at www.kimberlykayeterry.com.

To Love a
WILDE

Kimberly Kaye Terry

KIMANI™
ROMANCE

KIMANI PRESS™

Recycling programs for this product may not exist in your area.

ISBN-13: 978-0-373-86205-4

TO LOVE A WILDE

Copyright © 2011 by Kimberly Kaye Terry

www.kimanipress.com

Printed in U.S.A.

Dear Reader,

Writing Jasmine and Holt's story, the second book in the Wyoming Wilde family miniseries, was rewarding, but often challenging! As I wrote their story and saw them coming to vivid life, these two characters were, at times, fun, sexy and completely irreverent. Other times they were stubborn and obstinate. They are two people who are bound and determined not to succumb to what everyone around them can see is inevitable—that they are falling in love. Hard.

What started off as a simple story of a woman who fell in love with a man, became one that was boundary-pushing and unpredictable, but always a hot, wild and amazing love story.

I hope you enjoy reading Jasmine and Holt's story as much as I enjoyed writing it!

As always, keep it sexy ;)

Kimberly Kaye Terry

Chapter 1

"Are you okay, baby? Is the rope too tight?"

Hot liquid eased down her inner thighs in response to the words whispered coarsely against her neck.

"No." She paused and drew in a breath. "They're… they're not too tight, I mean. I…I'm okay." She stammered out the response.

"Good."

One word and he had her going crazy.

Yasmine's head tossed on the pillow, her lids tightly closed and her breath coming out in hitched puffs of air as she eagerly waited to feel his mouth against hers and his big body blanket her, forcing her farther down on the mattress.

"But you have to tell me, baby."

She shivered as the whispered words feathered

along her neck. Her body bowed, arching toward him, desperate to meet his scalding-hot touch.

"Tell you…tell you what?" she panted, groaning when he captured the lobe of her ear with his teeth and tugged.

"You know what I want to hear." He licked the side of her neck with his tongue.

She felt his hand skim up her thigh, past her hip, over her waist and up the midline of her body before he cupped one of her breasts in his big hand, strumming his thumb over her nipple until it tightened against his palm.

"Tell me, Yas." He drawled the words against her ear in a voice so deep it sent shivers dancing along her spine. The breath that fanned the hair at her temple made her draw in a ragged breath.

Even as she arched into his embrace, ready to tell him whatever it was he wanted to hear, to end the sensual storm that raced in her body, the same one that had been burning for ten years, a nagging buzz in the distance distracted her, refusing to go away.

In frustration she raised a hand, surprised at the ease with which she removed it from the ropes binding her wrists together, and batted away at thin air, as though to make the noise go away.

It grew louder, more insistent. She opened her mouth, ready to tell him whatever he needed to hear, to tell him how she really felt about him, the way she'd felt about him since the first time she'd met him, when she was no more than a child. Ready to tell him that as much as she'd tried to let go and move on with her life, thoughts of him were always there, in the back of her mind, hovering…but the buzz grew so loud and strident Yasmine knew she couldn't ignore it any longer.

Her eyes flew open.

With a cry of disappointment and pent-up frustration, she glared up at the ceiling, her heart pounding and sweat trickling down the valley between her breasts.

She didn't have to look around to see if she was alone. She already knew.

She'd had yet another wake-me-up-before-I-go-go dream, featuring none other than Holt Wilde. Another scalding-hot dream where yet again she'd awakened horny, frustrated. And all alone.

"Don't forget that part," she mumbled aloud in self-disgust. "Seems like I've been alone my entire life."

She shook her head in a feeble attempt to dispel the lingering images of the two of them locked in an embrace so hot she felt her cheeks burn. She swallowed deeply, placing her palms over her burning face.

She'd traveled the world, studied with some of the world's best chefs, and now, after her stunning win of a televised major culinary competition, she was able to see her lifelong dream of owning her own upscale restaurant come to life.

Her life now was *exactly* as she dreamed it would be and more.

She had no time in her life for adolescent dreams. Now wasn't the time to allow ghosts from her past to enter her life. Even if the ghost was six-feet-plus of raw masculinity that had filled enough dreams to last her a lifetime.

At any rate, it wasn't as though she had now or ever occupied his thoughts the way he had hers. The man didn't even know she was alive.

"Time to face the world…seize the moment, and all that jazz," she mumbled, purposely infusing energy and optimism into her voice, reciting her favorite mantra. Even to her own ears, her voice was flat.

Yasmine rose from bed and stuffed her feet inside her slippers before making her way to the bathroom.

Just as she was turning on the showerhead, the phone rang. After glancing at the clock, seeing the early hour, she was seconds away from ignoring it, thinking it was just some telemarketer. Saturday mornings seemed to be their M.O. for calling her, nine times out of ten. But with everything going on in her life over the past few months, she didn't want to chance missing an important call.

Grabbing the bath towel from the hook near the shower door she hastily wrapped it around her body, walked over and snatched up the phone.

"How's my baby girl doing this morning?" A familiar voice spoke into the phone, and with a small smile, Yasmine plopped back down on the sofa that also served as her bed. "I called you earlier, but you weren't home. Did you get my message?"

"I'm doing great, Aunt Lilly, definitely can't complain! And, no, I haven't had a chance to check my voice messages, I'm sorry. How are you?" she answered, a smile on her face.

"I'm fine, baby. And so proud of you I could just about pop! I got the magazine in the mail yesterday and almost hurt myself running around showing everyone my baby!" she enthused, and Yasmine laughed outright.

She'd sent her aunt a copy of a top culinary magazine and the one that sponsored the Top Young Chef competition she'd recently won. That month's issue featured Yasmine on the cover, trophy in hand, along with a two-page spread inside highlighting Yasmine's win of the competition.

"I went to town yesterday, and, baby, I must have bought out every copy of the magazine they had at the local Walmart! I even had one of the articles with your picture framed and mounted!" she said, and Yasmine could hear the pride oozing from her voice.

Yasmine sat back on the bed, her smile growing as she listened to her aunt's glowing praise. She herself was still reeling from it all and was having a hard time believing how her life had changed so dramatically, particularly over the last month.

"Aunt Lilly, half the time I feel like pinching myself to make sure this isn't all some dream," she said, laughing. "I still can't believe it all."

"Well, believe it, baby. You worked hard for it, and deserve every bit of happiness life can give you. I'm happy that I had a small bit to do with that."

"You had more than a little to do with it, Aunt Lilly. I don't know what I would have done without you, during the competition as well as my entire life," she said softly, and both women were silent for a moment.

"Enough about me, how are you doing? Everything going well on the ranch? Anything new and exciting happening?" Yasmine said, injecting a cheerful note into her voice.

"Yes, it's all going well, baby. Same ole, same ole, as they say," Lilly said, lightly laughing before pausing and clearing her throat. "Well, with the exception of planning the wedding."

At that, Yasmine's hand gripped the receiver tighter. "Wedding? What wedding? Who's getting married?" Her stomach fell when her aunt didn't immediately respond, and she sat up straight in the bed, her hand tightening on the phone.

"Who's getting married, Mama Lilly?" she asked, reverting to the name she unconsciously called her aunt whenever she grew upset.

"Nathan is, baby girl," Lily answered softly, knowing what caused Yasmine's reaction.

"Nate?" she asked, surprised.

"I'm as shocked as you are." Lily laughed and continued, "We all are." She went on to fill Yasmine in on the story. As she listened, Yasmine unconsciously blew out a breath of air, closing her eyes, the knot of anxiety in her stomach easing away.

"I hope I'm invited to the wedding," she said hesitantly.

"Of course, Yasmine, you're family!"

There was another short pause. This time she distinctly heard her aunt expel a long breath, making her frown.

"What is it, Aunt Lilly? Spill. What's going on that you're not telling me?"

"Nothing's going on, baby, what are you talking about? I just was thinking, that's all."

"About?"

Although Yasmine loved her aunt like a mother, there were times when she wanted to scream in frustration when trying to pry something out of her, particularly if it would make her aunt worry. This was one of those times. The fact that her aunt had called her twice in the same day should have alerted Yasmine that something was going on.

"Well, I didn't want to worry you. But it seems as though I'm going to have to have surgery," Lilly finally said, and Yasmine sat straight up, the knot of dread returning, this time for her aunt.

"Surgery? What type of surgery? What do you mean surgery? When? What are you talking about, Aunt Lilly? Why are you just now telling me?" She asked the questions in back-to-back succession.

"Baby, calm down! Listen…it's nothing major, I—"

"No big deal? How can you say that? Wha—"

"If you would let me finish," Lilly broke in, and Yasmine stopped and drew in a breath.

"Like I said, it's not major. You know how bad my knees are. This time it's my right knee. It's going out on me again. Docs want to give me another knee-joint replacement."

"Another one? You just had that one—"

"Fifteen years ago, Yas." Lilly again broke in. "Just a few years before you came to live with me, baby," she said, chuckling softly.

"Oh," Yasmine replied, sitting back on the sofa, her body slumping.

Time had flown by. It seemed like yesterday she'd come to live with her aunt after her parents had dropped her off, unable…or unwilling…to take her with them as they went off on one of their "grand adventures." Although she missed her parents when she was sent to her aunt's, she'd later be thankful, as Lily had become a second mother to her after her parents died in a plane crash.

Yasmine expelled a long, relieved breath. Although she preferred her aunt didn't have to have any type of surgery, this was one she could handle. "Who's going to take care of your 'boys' while you're recuperating?" she said, and heard Lilly's husky, soft laugh again.

Lilly never made it a secret how much she loved the Wildes…or her boys, as most, including Yasmine, referred to them.

After Jed Wilde had adopted the boys formally, he had hired Lilly on as the housekeeper to do light cleaning and to cook for his new family and the ranch hands he employed, as well. Eventually she'd moved in with the family, living in the home with them, and had become much more than an employee. She'd become family.

When Yasmine had shown up on her doorstep after the death of her parents, not only had Lilly welcomed her, so had Jed and his adopted sons.

Lilly had always treated her as though she was the daughter she'd never had, loved and cared for her, fussed at her when she needed it. She was the mother Yasmine had always wanted, and she couldn't have asked for a better parent.

But for her to ask her to come back to the ranch, face Holt again, was something she didn't think she could do, not even for her aunt.

"Baby…I need you," Lilly said.

And just like that, she had her.

With a barely suppressed groan, Yasmine agreed.

Chapter 2

Yasmine brushed away the hair that had escaped the tight chignon she'd so meticulously created that morning with one hand as she dragged her wheeled suitcase behind her with the other, avoiding passengers as she hurried along the airport terminal.

Her stomach rolled, reminding her that she hadn't eaten since early that morning, and that had been nothing more than a bran muffin and a cup of coffee before she headed out to the airport.

But she knew it wasn't the lack of food that was making her stomach grumble or giving her the overall queasy feeling in her gut. No, lack of food had nothing to do with her current state. To say she was on edge was putting it mildly.

Soon after assuring her aunt that she'd come home,

she'd gotten in touch with the producer from the popular food and cooking network. After winning the reality-show competition, she'd been approached to host her own show, and like everything else, it was a dream come true for Yasmine.

But her aunt needed her and there was no way she could turn away from helping. Relieved, she was told that the show was still in the development stage and they needed to iron out details, such as the location and theme of the show. Although she hadn't signed a formal contract, she was assured they were still very much interested in her and that her six-week absence would be acceptable. By that time, they would have everything ready, and she could do the first taping.

Relieved, she'd scratched one thing off of her to-do list and made the second call, this one to Clayton Moore, the owner of some of the most upscale restaurants in New York, who'd also approached her for the position as executive chef at one of his restaurants.

"Of course! *Absolutely* that's no problem, Yas!" he'd assured her to her relief, when she'd asked if she could have more time to think about his offer and told him of her aunt's need for her.

Although she'd felt the slightest bit uncomfortable with him using the shortened version of her name, she brushed it off, listening intently as he continued. "I told you, I'm very much interested in you…working for me, that is," he'd said, quickly clarifying, making her unease escalate.

After her win of the show and the subsequent media

attention, to Yasmine's astonishment the offers had come pouring in from all directions. From requests to pitch a "miracle" dicer and slicer on one of the shopping networks to pitchwoman for a local down-home fast-food joint, the offers had been coming regularly.

"You take care of what you need to, and I'll see you in a few weeks. And remember, I'm just a phone call away. In fact, before you head out, if you have time, I'd love to bring you by the restaurant, maybe have dinner. And discuss anything you might have questions about?" he'd asked, and Yasmine could feel his big smile come through the phone.

Something about his smile reminded her of the wolf in "Little Red Riding Hood." And she definitely was beginning to feel like Little Red herself when, after the first meeting, his assessing glance brushed over her, subtly but with enough attention that she grew uncomfortable.

She'd shaken off the feeling when the rest of the meeting had gone smoothly and he hadn't been in the least bit unprofessional.

Clayton Moore was definitely a mover and shaker in the restaurant business, and for him to offer Yasmine such a coveted position, as executive chef with two sous-chefs of her own, along with a full kitchen crew, was beyond remarkable.

Although she'd planned to use her earnings and newfound notoriety to open her own restaurant, the offer was more than appealing. If she accepted it, she'd be one of the youngest chefs to attain such a lauded position.

As for Clayton…Yasmine was more than aware that he was interested in offering her something more than a job. From the moment they'd met, the handsome entrepreneur had made his interest known.

Tall, dark, handsome and sophisticated. Clayton Moore was everything she *should* want in a man.

The minute Clayton's face came to her mind, another man's image superimposed its way over his. Forced its way in. Arrogantly shoved the other man's image away as though he had every right to, Yasmine thought in irrational irritation.

Holt Wilde, the youngest of the Wilde men.

And each time it did, she ruthlessly shoved away the image of his big, hard body, along with the Stetson he always wore low, shadowing his bright blue eyes and hiding that half smile he seemed to favor…the one that always gave her shivers even when it *wasn't* directed at her.

It wasn't as though he was forcing her to think of him. In fact, she doubted she herself ever came to his mind.

Maybe that was what was more irritating than anything else, Yasmine thought glumly. The fact that she alone had this obsession with a man who probably didn't even remember her, much less think of her on a regular basis, like clockwork, as she had him, all these years.

"I need *serious* intervention," she mumbled aloud. "One-on-one, put me in the prayer circle and douse me with holy water type of intervention."

Out of her peripheral vision Yasmine saw a young

mother tug her toddler closer toward her, eyeing Yasmine with a frown on her face.

There she went again, talking out loud. Ugly habit she had, whenever anything plagued her.

"And Holt Wilde is just one big old plague," she said out loud, again.

This time the woman grabbed her child's hand and hurried in the opposite direction from Yasmine.

She ignored the woman and straightened her shoulders as she continued to stride through the airport. But no more.

No, she was determined that by the end of her stay at the ranch, things would change, she'd make sure of it. While helping her aunt, she had another agenda in mind. She would, once and for all, exorcise all thoughts and fantasies of the one man who had invaded her mind for nearly twenty years, rid herself of the feelings, feelings she knew were simply a residue of her girlhood crush, once and for all.

This time she would be the one to walk away…

Holt bit back a curse as he waited impatiently for the van packed full of tourists to move along. The uniformed police officer who whistled and waved his baton in front of the double-parked van in front of the airport was about as effective as an ass on a gnat, Holt thought, his irritation escalating.

Apprehension had his damn guts tied in knots, which didn't help his current situation.

When his brother had asked him to pick up Lilly's

niece, Yasmine, from the airport, to say it was the last thing he wanted to do was putting it mildly. It was Sunday, the day he and his brothers, as well as the rest of the ranch hands, took it easy, the day they all attended to their own interests.

He thought back on his interest. That would be the blonde beauty he'd left in bed curled up around his pillow earlier that morning after he'd received the call from his brother Nate.

All thoughts of going another round with the woman came to a screeching halt when Nate had informed him that their housekeeper, Lilly, a woman they viewed more as a mother than an employee, needed a favor.

With her surgery coming up, the doctor had ordered as much rest for Lilly as possible, and the hour-and-a-half drive to pick her niece up from the airport wasn't something she could manage.

He'd sat straight up in bed, impatiently shoving the hair from his eyes as he'd listened while his brother blithely went on to tell him that Holt needed to pick Yasmine up from the airport, as no one else was available.

Holt's thick brows came together in a deep frown as he inched along the congested traffic at the airport, remembering the conversation.

"No one else can get her?" He'd questioned his oldest brother while glancing down at the woman who lay cuddled close to him, sound asleep in bed. "What about Jake? Last I knew he was staying at the ranch more than he was in town. Can't he pick her up?"

Momentarily distracted, he saw her move... He frowned, trying to think of the woman's name... Amy. Amy inched closer to him, the sheet covering her slim body slipping down to reveal one of her small, plump breasts. Before the call, that would have been more than enough enticement for Holt to awaken the sleepy woman and go at it another round.

But that was before he found out that Yasmine was returning. Now the image of the young girl he'd known long ago filled his mind.

"Payback can be a bitch, bro."

"Asshat," he'd bitten out as Nate's booming laugh echoed into the phone, stabbing the end button on his cell and staring down at the phone, a deep frown on his face.

Nate was his oldest brother and had recently become engaged. The fact that Holt, along with their middle brother, Shilah, had hired Althea knowing Nate's mandate of no women allowed had been an issue. Even though it had turned out well—better than that, the two of them had fallen head over heels in love, despite Nate's avowals of never wanting to get married—both Holt and Shilah had known that he'd get them back for their interference.

Everyone knew, Holt included, that as a young girl Yasmine had had a major crush on him. Although he'd not allowed himself to think of her in romantic terms back then, he easily recalled her big brown eyes and riotous mane of curls and her laugh... The sound of her laugh had always made him pause.

"Round one goes to you, big brother, but the game ain't over," he'd said to the empty phone.

Holt had tossed the phone on the side table. The woman—hell, what was her name?—had sleepily turned to him at that moment, reaching out for him. He'd given her a distracted smile and kissed her on the forehead, promising to see her later in the week, that something had come up at the ranch, and within a matter of minutes he'd dressed and had headed out.

He'd planned to park and go inside to help Yasmine with her bags, but a last-minute change in the airport she was scheduled to fly into had made it so that he had barely got there in time for her plane to land. His glance fell to the dashboard. According to the flight itinerary she'd texted to Miss Lilly, she would have made it in thirty minutes ago.

There had always been something about Yasmine that made him want to go the other way whenever he was around her.

He remembered when she first came to the ranch; she couldn't have been any older than nine or ten to his twelve years of age. He remembered that she rarely spoke; in fact, he'd wondered if she could until finally he had heard her laugh while in the kitchen with her aunt.

Her laughter, even back then, had drawn him to her, and briefly mesmerized, he'd stood in the doorway, staring across at her. But the minute she saw him, her light brown face flushed with color and she literally flew from the kitchen.

It hadn't taken long for Holt to realize, as they grew older, that she had a crush on him.

That crush came to an awkward head when, the day before Holt left for college, the young Yasmine grabbed him and pulled him close and kissed him. Surprised, he'd pulled away. But not before he'd returned the kiss for a short time. The memory of her soft lips, the feel of her soft young curves against him, had intermittently whispered into his mind throughout the years.

That was the last time he'd seen her.

When he'd returned home, Yasmine had always been away, and within two years she had left for culinary school. The few times she'd come to visit her aunt, she'd always managed to come when he wasn't home, whether by accident or design, Holt never knew.

Finally, the van moved and he scanned the crowded throng, looking for her.

He drew in a breath and froze, his hands gripping the steering wheel like a vise, his eyes widening, then narrowing. He felt as if he'd been sucker punched right in the gut.

Although it had been years since he'd seen her last, he knew the minute he saw the woman standing near the curb that it was her.

Yasmine Taylor. All grown up.

Damn.

The traffic and noise from the bustling travelers, the irritating shrill whistle from the cop, all faded to background noise as he sat behind the wheel, transfixed, staring at her.

The sun's rays gleamed against her upswept dark brown hair.

His gaze swept over her, head to toe.

She was small; he remembered that she'd barely reached him at chest level as a young girl. She'd been slightly overweight when she was younger. However, as an adult, the curves had settled in all the right places, he thought, subtly adjusting his jeans, the fit becoming uncomfortable as he watched her bend over and unzip a compartment in her luggage.

Her jeans hugged her firm, round bottom to a T, and as she bent forward, the ends of the shirt she wore, which hugged her generous breasts, slipped out of her waistband, exposing the slim expanse of unblemished brown skin.

When she straightened she looked directly at him, her large, doelike eyes widening. Even from his ten yards' distance away from her, he could see the flush that blazed across her face.

Again, he felt his gut clench and his mouth go dry as she stood staring at him, across the walkway.

The shrilling whistle broke him out of his absorption and he broke his gaze, turning to see the cop maniacally waving his baton, urging him forward.

"Sorry about that." Yasmine glanced behind her, mumbling the apology when her suitcase banged against the guy standing so close behind her she could almost feel his warm breath singe the back of her neck.

But really, did he have to jump into the same sliding

door as she had, at the same time? Plastering a fake smile on her face while pushing as close as humanly possible against the glass-paned door, she heaved a big sigh of relief when she finally tumbled out, nearly falling when the man pushed past her.

It was an unseasonably warm day, particularly for Wyoming, and she felt a trickle of sweat travel past her forehead and down the side of her face as she emerged from the revolving doorway. She righted herself and brushed her hands over her hips, down her jeans, a scowl on her face, as she scanned the curbside, looking for the ranch's foreman, Jake Stone.

As soon as she'd deboarded the plan she'd turned on her cell and checked her messages. Earlier she'd made a hasty call to her aunt when she'd learned the plane she was scheduled to fly on was having mechanical issues.

Because of that, instead of flying into the nearby airport, she'd had to travel into this one, nearly four hours away from the ranch.

She'd been disappointed when she'd heard the message from her aunt, telling her she wouldn't be able to pick her up from the airport, that her knee had been bothering her and she was instead sending the foreman from the ranch.

She'd been looking forward to the alone time with her aunt, to catch up on life on the ranch since the last time she visited. Although it had been a few years since she'd seen Jake, she found herself smiling, her mood lightened. Jake had always had a way of putting her at ease. Even when she was a younger woman, when she was so painfully shy, he could drag a smile out of her.

He was as much a part of Wilde Ranch as the men who owned it, as his father was Jed Wilde's first foreman. Jake had grown up at the ranch from boyhood and eventually he'd taken over the position as foreman when his father retired.

And besides, the man knew how to make a great lemon Bundt cake. Any guy who could make a lemon Bundt, much less from scratch, was a winner in her book.

Yasmine shook her head, a ghost of a smile on her face as she thought of the ranch. It had been a long time since she'd visited, and she'd found herself eager to come home the closer the time came for her departure. Everyone who worked at the Wilde Ranch was treated like family. From the first moment she'd come, she'd been welcomed. Jed Wilde had been that type of man. Despite his gruff outer demeanor, he had a heart of gold and did his best to make her feel at home.

And as she inhaled a deep breath, releasing it slowly, Yasmine realized that she'd missed home.

The last time she'd been to the ranch had been after graduating from culinary school in Chicago, before she'd moved to Paris to study. Many times her aunt had requested she come and visit, but nine times out of ten, Yasmine found an excuse not to, and without questioning her reasons, her aunt would come to visit her instead.

They both knew the reason for her reluctance: Holt Wilde. But she was no longer that pudgy, shy adolescent who pined for the young rancher. She'd traveled the world, she'd already accomplished much of what she'd dreamed of and her future was only looking better.

She was a woman who was self-assured, confident and one who most definitely did not have any residual feelings for Holt Wilde.

She ignored the mocking inner laugh and put a determined smile on her face when she saw the red pickup with the ranch's logo emblazoned on the side parked curbside. She waved, hoping Jake would see her, and quickly leaned down to unzip her bag and deposit her jacket before rising

She'd made it to within a few feet of him when she came to a sudden and complete halt, her eyes widening, her mouth opened.

She frowned, her heart racing as she squinted her eyes, thinking they were fooling her, that the man behind the wheel couldn't be…

No, she wasn't ready, she thought, her heart kicking viciously as she watched him pull smoothly to the curb and jump out.

Oh God, yes, it was. She swallowed deep, her glance running over him, from his large feet wearing scuffed cowboy boots, up thick, muscled thighs that bulged beneath the jeans he wore, over the denim jacket until she reached the bright blue gaze that haunted her dreams.

"It's been a while, Yas… Good to see you come home again," he said, his deep baritone voice brushing over her, sending hot shivers throughout her body. When he reached a hand out for her to take, she stared down at it, her mind scrambled, unable to gather her wits enough to figure out what in the world to do.

Chapter 3

"Traffic doesn't seem too bad. The ride should take us less than four hours," Holt murmured, sliding a glance toward Yasmine as he took the exit that would lead to the ranch.

Her creamy, light brown skin had a natural, healthy glow, one that required no makeup to enhance.

Her round cheeks of adolescence had narrowed, making her large brown eyes, slightly tilted at the corners, dominate her face. He didn't remember them being so beautiful. Her nose was small, and her lips...damn, her lips could keep a man up late at night, his mind conjuring up all kinds of sinfully delightful things he could do with them.

He subtly adjusted his body in the seat, his jeans

becoming painfully tight as the images slammed into his mind, ones he ruthlessly forced away.

And the way she smelled... Damn, did she have to smell so good? he thought with an inward groan. Her scent was pure intoxication; a mixture of a light floral, along with her own natural scent, had created a tantalizing smell that no perfume manufacturer could create on their best day.

But it wasn't just her scent that was driving him crazy. Added to that was the quiet yet sexy confidence she exuded, one that both puzzled him and drew him in at the same time, both feelings making him feel like a gauche schoolboy out on his first date.

Yasmine kept her gaze firmly out of the side window, afraid that if she looked back at Holt, she'd do something crazy like grab him, pull him toward her and kiss him directly on his sexy mouth.

She drew in a deep breath and expelled it slowly, his light aftershave and natural scent blowing across her senses like the air from a fan on a warm summer day.

She snuck a peek at him from beneath lowered lashes.

When he'd picked her up from the airport it had taken all she had inside her not to do just that, grab the man and kiss him.

As a woman this time and not a girl, Yasmine thought, remembering their first and only kiss.

It had been right before he was leaving for college. When she'd first come to the ranch after her parents died, she'd immediately clung to her aunt, who'd been her father's sister. Too shy to speak to anyone besides Lilly, it hadn't been long before she'd felt welcomed into the Wilde family. Some of her shyness had begun to wear off and she felt comfortable around the family, as well as those who worked the ranch.

All except for Holt. From the moment she first met him, she'd been mesmerized by him. Their age difference had been only three years, yet he seemed so much more...older, more sure of himself. Of all the Wilde men, Holt was the most outgoing. She shook her head in memory. He was the most outrageous.

As they grew older, she remembered her aunt laughing at some of his antics, claiming Holt could charm the honey from a queen bee.

Not that he'd ever flirted with her, she thought, stealing a glance at him as he drove, his strong hands lightly resting on the steering wheel. At best he treated her as little more than a younger sister, and even then he barely spoke to her.

She glanced away, turning her attention back to the window, blindly watching the landscape as they sped down the two-lane highway.

No, with her he was always polite, yet she'd always felt as though he'd held her at a distance. That feeling only grew as they got older. Whenever she was around, Holt always seemed to find a reason to leave the room. Often, it left her feeling confused, embarrassed and hurt all at once.

But that didn't stop the crush she had on him the size of the Teton Mountains from growing.

Once she'd followed him to one of the barns after seeing him come home late at night. It had been the week before he was leaving for college. She'd snuck inside and although she knew what she was doing was wrong, she peeked through a hole in the stable where he'd taken the girl he'd come home with.

She'd drawn in a deep breath when she saw Holt and the girl locked in an embrace, her blouse off and skirt hiked up as he was moments away from making love to her. He must have heard the sound, because he pulled away from the girl and glanced around, his features pinched.

Embarrassed and afraid she'd get caught, she'd quietly fled the stable, but not before she heard the girl's entreaty that he return and the soft giggles that turned to moans as he quickly picked up where he'd left off before being interrupted.

That same night Yasmine stayed up, images of Holt and the half-naked girl plaguing her mind, until finally she'd sat up in bed, determined to tell him how she felt, unable to keep her feelings to herself.

She'd opened the door, not exactly sure what she was going to do, when he was walking down the hallway, a towel wrapped around his lean hips.

Yasmine gulped, her eyes rolling over the length of his hard naked chest that even then showed the promise of the man he'd become.

He'd smiled at her, subtly adjusting the towel, and asked what she was doing up so late.

She'd stuttered, making idle chat, before shyly telling him she was going to miss him when he left for school. She'd smiled, stuck out her chest in her best imitation of Amanda, the girl he'd taken to the barn, and leaned against the door, trying her best to appear sexy but knowing she was failing miserably.

His smile had slipped and Yasmine knew she should just stop, go back inside her room and abandon her plan. But she didn't.

This was the last time she'd probably have alone with him before he left. If she didn't tell him how she felt now, she didn't think she'd ever be able to summon the courage to do it.

It was now or never, she'd thought.

"I'll miss you, too, Yas," he'd said, drawing nearer. He placed his hand on top of her head as though to ruffle her hair. For some reason that was the impetus she needed to show him she wasn't a kid anymore.

At that moment, she'd grabbed him, pulled him inside her bedroom and kissed him with all the passion and longing she'd had building up for him for six years.

At first he'd been still as a statue, but a moment before he broke free, she felt his lips soften and a hint of a response. He'd wrapped his arm around her waist and dug deeply into the skin, the thin, flimsy nightshirt she wore riding up enough that the heat from his palm scorched the skin on her back. The kiss lasted little longer than a few seconds before he'd broken free, a deep frown settling over his handsome, chiseled features.

Yasmine had been so embarrassed she'd wanted to crawl up into a hole somewhere and die. She didn't need him to say a word—the look on his face, a mixture of anger and pity, said it all.

She stumbled away and spun around, hoping to God he'd just leave and not say anything to her. Just leave. She felt a hand on her shoulder and swallowed down the melon-ball lump that had gathered in her gut and turned to face him.

"Yasmine, I—"

She held up a hand, stopping him before he could continue, and forced a trembling smile on her face. "I'm sorry, Holt, I don't know what came over me... Can we just forget that I did that? Please?" The last word was barely above a whisper. She was so choked up with embarrassment she simply wanted him to go away.

His eyes searched hers, concern darkening his blue eyes to a smoky gray. With a nod he patted her awkwardly on the shoulder and left her room.

As soon as he did, Yasmine, in true teenage-girl form, full-on angst, cried herself to sleep.

The next day, Jed packed up the truck and he and Holt headed off to get him settled into the dorms.

That was the last time Yasmine was ever alone with Holt.

Since then, on the occasions she came to visit her aunt, she made sure that Holt was nowhere around. Anything else would have been too mortifying.

Yasmine settled back in the seat, and unable to resist, again cast Holt a sideways glance.

When he'd taken her bags at the airport, she'd caught the way his glance had stolen over her and had barely refrained from patting her hair and checking her makeup. Tall, he stood at least a foot taller than she. Thankfully she'd opted to wear heels traveling, giving her the added inches so she at least didn't have to crane her neck to see his face.

He hadn't removed his Stetson when he greeted her, and glancing up at him, her breath had caught at the back of her throat, as he was a living, breathing poster boy for raw, masculine cowboy if she ever saw one.

Lord, the man was fine, she thought, expelling a long breath while mentally reciting over and over that she was an adult and no longer an adolescent with a schoolgirl's crush.

When he'd turned toward her after placing her luggage in the back, her self-affirming mantra reminding her of her sophistication flew right on out the window, and she felt like the shy, adolescent she had once been all over again.

The fact that he had been checking her out just as much as she had him hadn't escaped her attention. That had been just enough to boost her confidence and make her realize that *she* was the one in control.

But in no way was she going to delude herself into thinking anything more of his casual appraisal than what it was. She was well aware of her attributes, without conceit. Although not as beautiful as the women he dated, she felt confident in the way she looked. She knew she'd changed some in both looks and attitude, grown up a lot, since the last time he had seen her, and the change no doubt was one he noticed. But that's all it was.

She inched closer to the door.

And he was in for a big surprise if he thought she still held on to that silly schoolgirl crush.

Chapter 4

"Do you like what you see?" Holt asked Yasmine, as she'd been staring out of the truck's passenger window for several moments.

Immediately he felt like an idiot, trying to come up with some lame attempt at conversation. In his desire to find something clever to say, to keep their conversation going, his mind had gone blank, the only thing surfacing being about the weather.

If his brothers could see him now, the self-proclaimed love doctor fumbling trying to come up with conversation, they'd break their necks falling out laughing at him.

"The weather, I mean," he clarified, clearing his throat when she lifted one brow in question.

A small smile tilted the corners of her generous

mouth upward before she nodded. His eyes trained on the small dimple that flashed when she smiled. "I do. It's beautiful out. Nothing like the weather-channel prediction I got before I headed out this morning."

"Yeah, I think I saw that. Uh, on the weather channel, that is. About the forecast and it being a cold day," he said and promptly clamped his mouth shut when he saw the humor lighting her dark brown eyes.

Real smooth, Wilde, he thought, inwardly kicking himself in the ass. He didn't know the last time, if ever, a woman had reduced him to a stumbling boy. He quickly turned his attention back to the road.

"Has it been nice like this for long? I remember how cold it can get sometimes this time of year."

"We've had a good winter. Nothing like New York, though, I bet," he'd said and when she lifted another brow, he hastily turned his attention back to the road. "That is where you're living these days, right? I, uh, think I remember Lilly mentioning that you had moved from Chicago to New York a few months ago."

In fact, he'd known exactly where Yasmine had been living, from the time she graduated from culinary school in Chicago and moved to study in Paris before settling back in Chicago. He'd followed her rise in the culinary world, read everything Lilly would so proudly show off to him and his brothers about Yasmine. He'd always chosen to ignore the fact that he'd always been aware of what she was doing, where she was living and the reason for it.

Holt knew it was a bad idea when his brother had

asked—scratch that—*told* him he had to pick Yasmine up from the airport. He also knew it was a bad idea the minute he saw her standing on the sidewalk waiting to be picked up.

But he had no idea how much he'd underestimated what a bad idea it was until he had her in his pickup, her luggage stored in the back and the two of them in his cab, her unique scent reaching out and grabbing him, pulling him up short.

He didn't remember her skin looking so soft, so clear and beautiful. Nor had he remembered the tendency she had to pull the full, lush bottom rim of her lips into her mouth, her thick brows coming together in a frown as she contemplated whatever it was she was thinking of.

There was something...different about her. To say she was pretty was too mild a description.

She'd lost the baby fat she'd carried as a younger woman, her face and body now slimmer, yet she'd held on to the curves. As he'd opened the door and helped her inside the cab of the truck, Holt's gaze had zeroed in like a torpedo to her backside. And damn, what a backside she had.

Although she was small in stature, the top of her head barely reaching him at chest level, she wore high heels that drew even more attention to her long legs. Her faded, ripped-up jeans cupped her firm buttocks with deadly, sexy precision, making his mouth go dry.

She'd removed her jacket and beneath it wore a simple button-up blouse, but there was nothing simple about the way the soft fabric molded and hugged her generous breasts. As she turned to thank him, he'd caught an up-close and personal view of them as the pretty brown skin swelled well above the V neckline of her shirt and pressed against the fabric. He caught a glimpse of the bow on the front of her bra when one of the straining buttons broke free.

She'd turned around and caught his gaze on her. Following his line of vision he saw her cheeks again blossom with color when she saw that her button had come undone. Fumbling, she'd hastily rebuttoned her blouse.

The fact that she'd blushed again made a part of him want to believe that blush was because of him, before he immediately dismissed the idea. She'd just been embarrassed that her blouse had come undone.

He'd been aware of her crush on him as a young woman, but there was no way the sexy, sophisticated woman she appeared to be now still held that same schoolgirl crush.

Beauty aside, Yasmine now exuded a sexy confidence, one that didn't jibe with his memories of the shy, clumsy girl he'd known long ago. One that made him even more aware of her than he ever had been back then, reminding him how as even a young girl there had always been something about her that had both attracted him to her and made him want to run the complete and opposite direction away from her.

Not that she had ever done anything to him to make him feel that way.

He turned to glance her way. She was staring out of

the passenger window, deep in thought. Nerves assaulted him, which made not one bit of damn sense. He'd known Yasmine since she was a young girl, when she'd moved to the ranch after her parents died. He remembered the day she first came and Jed had allowed Lilly to introduce her to the family.

She'd barely spoken a word, simply bobbed her head up and down as Lilly introduced her to the family. She'd solemnly shaken hands with his father and his brothers. When he struck out his hand to shake it, she'd only placed her hand in his for a brief moment before snatching it back as though she'd burned it. He'd caught the way her eyes had widened when they met his and the subtle way she'd wiped her palms down the side of the red-and-white gingham dress she wore.

A smile of remembrance split his face for a fraction of a moment before he frowned. The fact that he remembered what she wore, from the top of her plaited hair down to the old but polished Mary Jane shoes she wore surprised him.

"Lord, it's been a long time since I've seen that," she said, dragging him out of his thoughts. He turned and glanced out of the window. The stretch of the two-laned highway bordered a ranch, where in the distance cows were contently grazing.

"Don't see much of that where you live, I suppose," he said, and turned back to the road.

She laughed softly. "No, not really. Nothing but glass and buildings, bustling people and everybody is always busy… There's never a dull moment."

There was a short pause before he continued.

"Do you ever miss it? Ranch life, I mean," he asked. "Does all that…busyness get too much?"

He felt her gaze on him before she sighed softly. "I do sometimes. Miss the ranch. Mostly I miss the quiet," she replied, her voice soft. Although Holt kept his focus on the road as she continued, he listened attentively to her. There was something different about her, something indefinable. He wondered if and how much she'd changed from the sweet, shy girl she was the last time he'd spoken with her, nearly ten years ago.

"But I love the life I'm living. I enjoy what I do… the traveling, meeting new people, new adventures. My life is now what I always wanted it to be." She paused, then continued. "What I always dreamed it would be, anyway. Sometimes I have to pinch myself just to make sure it isn't just a dream," she said, laughing softly.

"I'm not surprised at all that you're successful, Yasmine. I remember even as a young girl you were always in the kitchen with your aunt, helping to cook. You always seemed at home there. And damn if some of the creations you came up with weren't some of the best cooking I've ever had," he complimented her, lightening the moment.

Yasmine laughed outright. "I guess you don't remember some of those hot-mess creations of mine, then?"

He chose that moment to glance her way and nearly hit the car in front of him. One side of her sensual, generous mouth hitched in a smile, and a deep dimple flashed in her cheek. He hastily turned his attention back to the road in front of him.

Ahead the two-lane road they were traveling had stilled due to construction. The road sign indicated it would be one lane for the next two miles, causing a small cluster of congestion. He turned back around to face her.

"Well, all I remember is what a fantastic chef you were. And I'm proud of you, Yas. We all are," he added, clearing his throat before continuing. "So tell me all about it. What was it like to win the competition?"

Her smile grew and her face became even more animated. "I swear I've never seen so many drama queens as I did during the taping of the show!" She laughed, and proceeded to fill him in on the behind-the-scenes action, which was much more drama-filled than what the camera crew had been able to capture. Not that they hadn't tried.

By the time she finished they were both laughing, and the earlier awkwardness evaporated. Yasmine went on to tell him how she felt the moment the competition heated, and she, along with the last two competitors, were the only ones left from the original twelve contestants.

As he inched along in traffic, Holt became caught up in simply watching her as she spoke, the way she used her hands to speak, the deep sparkle in her dark eyes, the way she nearly bounced in her seat, she was so animated. So much so that one of the buttons on her blouse threatened to slip free if she kept moving like that.

Holt firmly kept his eyes away from watching her chest and admiring the way her silk blouse clung and molded her generous breasts.

Damn, she most definitely had grown up, he thought.

"And now I hear you're going to be an executive chef at a famous restaurant? Starring in your own show, as well? That's got to be exciting. But like I said, I'm not surprised." He encouraged her to continue the conversation, enjoying listening to her, watching her animated face as the traffic all but stilled.

"That came out of the blue," she said, shaking her head, the smile still on her face. "The offer for my own show, that is. As far as the restaurant, it's something I've dreamed of. I just never thought it would happen this soon."

"Yeah, it seems like all of your dreams are coming true, Yas. And it's everything you deserve."

There was a slight lull as Yasmine sat back, the smile slipping from her face as she turned to him.

"God, I've spent the last hour talking about myself. I'm sorry!" she said, her cheeks flushing with color.

"No, I've enjoyed hearing about what you've been up to. It's been a long time since we've actually spoken. I like hearing about what's been going on in your world, Yas," he said.

It hit him that he hadn't realized how much he'd actually missed her, not really seeing her over the past ten years, and only hearing about her adventures through her aunt.

"I'm looking forward to getting reacquainted," he finished.

"Thank you," she murmured. Holt caught a hint of a blush steal across her cheeks when he risked a glance her way, capturing his attention before he forced himself to look away.

He hid a grin. So, he could still make her blush.

It was a start.

"So, Holt Magnum Wilde…what have you been up to?" she asked, and he heard the humor in her voice.

Holt had studiously avoided letting anyone know his middle name, only using his middle initial whenever he signed a document. It had always been a source of embarrassment. From what he'd gathered, his mother, at the time of his birth, had been enamored of an old television show featuring a character of the same name. Outside of his brothers, no one else knew what the middle initial stood for.

Well, with the exception of Miss Lilly and obviously Yasmine.

She laughed as he groaned, and Holt immediately felt an answering grin tug at the corners of his mouth at the sound of her tinkling laughter.

Once it died down he answered her question, infusing as much of a casual note into it as he could. "After Dad died my senior year in college, I came home for the summer and helped my brothers with the ranch. Things were hectic around the place for a while, but we pulled together, got everything back on target."

"I was sorry to hear about his death. He was a good

man," she said softly, placing her hand on his arm. Immediately she drew back.

He knew the gesture had been instinctive to her, she'd always been a warm person and didn't mean it as anything but a way to show comfort. But he felt the heat of her soft hand through his jacket as though she had made direct skin-to-skin contact, sending a jolt of electricity from his arm directly to his groin.

"Yeah, he was. He's still missed. The place isn't the same without him," he said, remembering the man he'd called father for nearly ten years. The only man he'd ever been able to call that name.

"I'm sure he would be proud of you…you and your brothers," she murmured, sympathy in her voice. "Proud of what you all have done with the ranch." She paused and lightly massaged his arm. It was all Holt could do to keep it together, keep his mind on the conversation.

He turned to her, his glance falling first to her hand and then to her blouse. The button that had been threatening to come loose had finally slipped free of the fastening, and he caught a peek of the lace that covered the crests of her breasts.

Taking his hand off the wheel briefly, he covered her hand, squeezed it, before casually removing it.

He wanted to curse when he saw the crestfallen look on her face, the way her cheeks again bloomed with color, this time, he knew, from embarrassment. He realized instantly she perceived his action as some kind of rejection. But damn if he could allow her to continue her innocent, yet stimulating, massage. Not without slamming into the car in front of them and causing an accident.

As it was, he was having a hard enough time keeping his erection in check around her, and had been since the moment he saw her bending over, her round little butt filling her jeans to perfection, and the peek he'd gotten of her slim waist as her shirt lifted away from the waistband of her jeans... He drew in a deep breath.

"Anyway, after that I returned to school, got drafted into the NFL and played professional football for a few years.

"Yes, I knew that...I mean, Mama Lilly mentioned you playing pro when you got drafted," she said, correcting herself.

Yasmine swallowed an embarrassed groan after he gently, yet firmly, removed her hand from his arm.

God, what had possessed her to touch him like that?

In all actuality she hadn't thought much about her actions, simply reached out to him...it had come so naturally. But, as soon as she had, she'd felt an electric heat sear her hand when she'd touched him.

And it didn't help matters in the least that her stupid blouse refused to stay closed. At that moment the button popped open, and the look in his eyes when he glanced down at her had made her treacherous nipples respond in kind. It was as though someone had kicked up the air-conditioning fifty degrees colder.

She'd ordered the shirt online, and hadn't tried it on

before donning it that morning, along with the just-as-useless new bra. Not that he'd believe her if she told him—he probably thought she'd worn the shirt on purpose, knowing it was a size too small.

And besides, even if she said anything, she'd feel even *more* foolish drawing more attention to the fact, she thought glumly.

As far as knowing what he'd been up to, well, she'd been well aware of Holt and his activities, at least the ones that seemed to make the news with the regularity that would make any one of the celebrity male sex symbols green with envy. He'd had his pick of women, beautiful women, from actresses and models to heiresses and famous female athletes.

His…exploits had been fodder for many a news outlet, particularly during his time playing pro ball.

Much as he'd been during the time she'd lived at the ranch, Holt Magnum Wilde was still a magnet to women. Beautiful, rich…sophisticated women.

Although he'd only played pro ball for three years before retiring, it seemed he was just as busy off the field as he was on the field.

In every photo she'd seen, he'd had a woman draped on his arm.

More often than not, two. Sometimes three.

Every time she'd glance and see his name mentioned in regards to a woman, Yasmine had subconsciously held her breath, waiting for the time when one of them proved to be more than a passing fling, yet they never had.

Even retired, although his exploits weren't as well advertised, the man still managed to make news. Nothing had changed.

As usual, with some woman on his arm, from the heiress he'd dated last year to the daughter of one of the most lucrative cattle farmers in Wyoming, he still had his pick from a bevy of women to choose from.

And although they'd seemed to click on the ride, and his interest in her life seemed real, he still saw her as nothing more than that little girl who'd had a crush on him.

Obviously nothing had changed about him in that regard, either.

She suppressed a sigh, planting the largest, fakest smile on her face that she could when he glanced her way, hoping he couldn't read her thoughts.

Chapter 5

"Ohhh…it's beautiful!" Yasmine sat up in her seat and rolled the window down, allowing the cool air to blow inside the truck. "It's been so long since I've been home!" She laughed, the sound tugging a smile from Holt as she leaned out the window to peer out as they sped past the outer reaches of the ranch.

After the construction zone ended, the rest of the trip had flown by and they'd made good time. Initially he'd imagined the drive as one he couldn't wait to get over; instead it had turned out to be one he wished could have lasted a lot longer. The time alone with her talking about old times was more enjoyable than any date he'd had in longer than he could remember.

The last fifteen minutes of the ride home had been made in silence, broken only by occasional idle conversation. The closer they came to the ranch, the more at ease Yasmine appeared. Relaxed.

Throughout the ride, even when they weren't speaking, Holt occasionally felt her gaze on him. He'd fought against the urge to turn her way and to broach the topic, the one thing that had been on his mind, hovering, since he was asked to pick her up from the airport. The event that had plagued his mind throughout the years, when he'd least expect it to. The night before he left for college and they kissed.

That night had changed the dynamics of their relationship. It had changed his view of her and for the first time made him aware of the fact that she wasn't a kid anymore.

He'd been aware of her crush on him…hell, everyone had, including his brothers, who had no problem teasing him over that fact through the years, to his embarrassment. It wasn't that he didn't like her, he did. But he saw her more as a family member, with Lilly being her aunt, rather than any romantic interest.

He tried avoiding her when her infatuation became obvious, hoping that would send the message to her, to no avail. Although she never actually said anything, the way she looked at him, the way she always seemed to be at the same place he was whenever he was working on the ranch, all told him she hadn't gotten the message.

As the years went by he'd begun to become even more aware of her. She was growing up, and growing up well, he thought, forcing himself to look away from her and give his attention to the road, before he ended up having an accident.

He'd told himself at the time the reason he started avoiding her was because of Yasmine. Yet he knew, deep down, that it was because of his own reaction to her. She was cute, shy, sweet and funny, and he found himself drawn to her. And she had the makings of a killer body, one that held promise, even then. A body that he knew good and damn well was off-limits to him.

Lilly would kick him or anyone else square in the tail if she so much as *thought* they were checking her "baby" out.

Holt respected Lilly and Yasmine too much, as well as fearing for his life, to ever consider flirting with the young girl. Lilly was as much of a mother to him as his own mother. More so, in fact.

"We'll be home soon."

She turned toward him, the smile on her face making his breath catch, and he bit back a groan.

It was *definitely* going to be an interesting visit.

No sooner had Holt opened her door for her before Yasmine was engulfed within her aunt's warm, tight embrace.

"I'm *so* happy to see you, baby girl! It's so good to have you home!"

Yasmine heard the strength of emotion clog her aunt's voice as she returned the tight hug, feeling the sting of tears burn her eyes as she held on to her aunt. They stood holding each other tightly, until finally, after long moments, Lilly released her. Placing her at arm's length, she ran a critical gaze over Yasmine, head to toe.

"And look at you! All grown up and looking beautiful… Baby, you're glowing!" she said, and Yasmine grinned, sniffing back the tears as she also took in her aunt, looking up at her.

Although she was in her mid-sixties, time seemed to have stood still for her aunt, Yasmine thought, blinking back the tears.

Her hair, mostly gray, was held back in a tight bun at the base of her head, bringing her strong, beautiful features into the spotlight.

Her aunt's dark eyes were widely spaced apart, like Yasmine's, with a hint of a slant in the corners, and her generous mouth, again like Yasmine's, usually was tilted up in a smile.

But that's where the similarities ended. Yasmine was much smaller in stature, with a tendency toward curves, whereas Lilly was tall and lean. With the exception of her boobs, Yasmine thought with a grin. Like Yasmine, her aunt had more than enough going on in that department to make up for her lack of curves anywhere else.

She recalled the way Holt had tried, unsuccessfully, to disguise the look in his eyes when he caught her struggling with the irritating button on her blouse.

The thought again brought a grin to her face. Despite the mixed signals he was sending her way, the man was interested, she thought, a small smile tilting the corners of her mouth up despite herself.

"And what's that smile for, girl?"

Her aunt was way too discerning. Nothing got past her. She had to remember that. If Aunt Lilly sniffed out the idea playing around in Yasmine's head, she'd be in a world of trouble.

"Nothing at all, Auntie...just happy to be home," she said, smiling up at her.

At that moment a shadow was cast above her, blocking out the late-afternoon sun. Yasmine didn't have to look over her shoulder to know who it was. The wave of goose bumps that feathered along her spine alerted her to who was behind her.

That and her aunt's slight frown as she looked from Yasmine to Holt, who stood directly behind her.

"The ride went well?" Lilly asked.

"It did!" Yasmine said, hooking her hand through the crook of her aunt's arm, linking them together.

"I'll take your things to the house, Yas."

She drew in a deep breath when he leaned close and his warm breath fanned the back of her neck before he grabbed her carry-on bag at her feet. He wrapped the long strap over his shoulder.

"I'm guessing these will go in Yas's old room?" he questioned her aunt, and she nodded her head yes.

Yasmine's hungry gaze followed him as he walked away, dragging her two wheeled bags behind him, his long-legged stride swiftly eating up the distance between the curved driveway and the house.

"Ahem..."

Yasmine was brought back to reality when her aunt coughed.

"So, does that sound good, baby girl? I know you don't like surprises."

She glanced at Lilly, trying not to blush at the way her aunt was eyeing her as though she had grown two horns and a tail. Lilly felt like a deer caught in the headlights; for the life of her, she didn't have a clue what her aunt had apparently asked her, she'd been so caught up in gazing at Holt.

"Uh, yeah. Sure, that sounds great, Aunt Lilly!" Yasmine decided to brazen it out. She injected as much enthusiasm into her voice as possible, not really sure what her aunt had said.

But as the frown slipped away from her aunt's face, replaced with a look of relief and a huge smile, Yasmine wondered what in the world she had just agreed to. She had a sneaky suspicion it was something she wouldn't have agreed to under normal circumstances.

Chapter 6

And she was right.

The minute she walked inside the ranch, she was greeted by a bevy of people, surprising her with a welcome-home gathering. Her eyes widened in surprise as she was crowded on all sides by those she'd known for years, and many she didn't. She recognized a few of the cowboys who, when she'd lived on the ranch, hadn't been much older than she was and now had children of their own.

As well, there were old familiars like Jake Stone, who enveloped her in a bear hug that rivaled her aunt's earlier embrace.

"It's been too long since you've been home, Yas! All grown up, too," Jake said, finally releasing her enough to run an appreciative glance over her that made her blush slightly.

"And, wow, look at you, Jake! I guess it's been longer than I thought since I've seen you," she said, grinning. "I don't remember you looking so…grown up," she said, running her own appreciative glance over his face.

He rubbed a hand over his well-trimmed beard and mustache. "You like?"

"I do!" she said, grinning up at him.

Yasmine glanced away, her smile still lingering, when she caught sight of Holt standing in a corner, near the granite stone fireplace. The smile slipped from her face when she noticed the tall blonde standing next to him, her manicured, French-tipped nails placed over his bulging biceps, her crimson-stained lips spread wide as she grinned up at Holt showing *all* thirty-two of her teeth.

His eyes met hers. Although the animated blonde with her death-grip hold on his arm was standing before him, his bright blue gaze was centered directly on Yasmine.

Even from across the room, she could feel the intensity of his stare. His gaze left hers, going to Jake, who still held her within his loose embrace.

When their eyes met again, she could feel the intensity of his stare from across the room. The energy between them was electric and seemed to sear her very flesh.

Disconcerted with the look, as well as the possessive hold the woman had on him, irritated for unknown reasons with both, Yasmine forced herself to look away, taking a deep breath, and upped the wattage on her smile to Jake.

"Hey, looks like you could use a refill... May I?"

Yasmine glanced down at her wineglass, which was now empty.

She frowned, not sure when she'd finished the glass. That was the second glass she'd had since the party started. Normally she kept it at a two-drink maximum, but she planned to enjoy her surprise party. "Sure, thanks. It's a celebration!" She agreed.

"You stay here, I'll be right back. Don't go anywhere. We still have a lot to catch up on, Yas," he said warmly.

"I'll be here," she replied with equal warmth.

As she watched him make his way through the crowded throng, Yasmine was helpless not to turn back in Holt's direction, only to find he was no longer in the same spot. She pushed back the odd disappointment. *What should it matter anyway where he'd gone?* she thought. Obviously her welcome-home party wasn't all that important. And if it wasn't important to him, it damn sure wasn't important to her if he stuck around or not.

The inner mocking laughter in her head was soon drowned out by two baritone voices saying her name.

"Yasmine...good to see you, girl! We've all missed you!"

Yasmine spun around, grinning ear to ear when both Nate and Shilah Wilde grabbed her and enveloped her in a group hug.

Squirming, sandwiched between the two big men, she laughed and pushed them away.

Close to Nate was a beautiful woman beaming at his side. Yasmine needed no introductions to know this had to be Althea, Nate's fiancée, from the look in her eyes as she gazed at him, along with the rock on her left hand that gleamed in the bright light.

After releasing her, he turned, placing a casual yet possessive arm around the woman and bringing her flush against his side.

He turned to Althea and made the introductions. Within moments of talking with her, Yasmine did a swift analysis and knew she was going to like the vivacious, lively woman.

When her aunt had first told her about Nate's upcoming nuptials, Yasmine had been more than curious to find out who'd won the heart of Nate Wilde, particularly after his disastrous first engagement. The Wildes were family to her, as close as she came to having brothers, and she couldn't stand the thought of him being hurt again.

After several moments of chatting, that thought was firmly put from her mind. The two were obviously madly in love, she thought, watching them as they stood with their arms wrapped around each other, talking to her.

When she saw the way the woman made Nate laugh, and the small, secret smiles they shared when they thought no one was looking, Nate whispering in her ear, whatever he said making her both giggle and blush, Yasmine felt a sting of jealousy for the love the two obviously shared before she quickly dispelled the feeling.

As the unofficial head of the household, Nate took his responsibilities seriously, always looking after the ranch, his brothers, as well as those who worked for them, putting their needs first. She smiled. He deserved happiness.

Jake soon returned and replaced her glass. For the next hour Yasmine talked and laughed with everyone, reacquainting herself with those she knew as well as forcing her natural reticence to the side and welcoming new faces.

"Looks like you're having a fantastic time, baby… So I'm forgiven?"

Yasmine turned and smiled as her aunt approached her.

"You most definitely are forgiven. I'm having a fantastic time," she replied happily.

Lilly raised one brow, a smile lingering around the corners of her wide mouth. She nodded her head toward Yasmine's empty glass. "I suppose after four of those, I'd be just as happy, too," she said, the sides of her mouth quirking.

"Four? I haven't had…" Yasmine stopped and laughed. She actually had lost count, caught up in the party mood and simply having a good time. "Were you keeping tabs on me, Aunty?"

"Always have. Probably always will" was Lilly's nonapologetic reply, and they both laughed. It was true.

And Yasmine wouldn't have it any other way. Her aunt's love and caring for her was a constant in her life, one she depended on.

"Yeah, I guess I've had enough of these. I'm afraid I've reached my limit," she agreed.

"You look beat," Lilly said bluntly. "Are you sure this isn't too much?"

"I am. But I'm having a great time." Although she was tired, having gotten up at zero-dark-thirty to catch her flight, she wasn't ready for the party to end. Something that surprised even her, as she normally wasn't the partygoing type.

"I think I'll just go outside for a bit. Catch some fresh air."

"Want me to go out with you?" her aunt asked, and Yasmine shook her head.

"No, I'll just go for a short bit, clear my head from these," she said and laughed. As much as she was enjoying herself and loved her aunt, Yasmine really did need a break from the festive party. Besides it being a long day, the excitement was starting to take its toll on her.

Her aunt gave her a quick hug. "Okay. You go ahead, baby. I'm sure no one will miss you for a short bit," Lilly said, and after a second quick hug, Yasmine left.

Lilly saw the minute Holt noticed Yas leave. The entire evening she'd watched the two as they circled around each other like a stallion and a broodmare in heat. Not coming too close to each other, but both aware of the other's presence.

Just as she guessed he would, within moments of Yasmine leaving, he quickly ended his conversation with the woman who'd been clinging to him like static the entire night, pawning her off on one of the young ranchers who willingly took the woman off his hands.

A small grin lifted the corners of Lilly's face. It was going to be one heck of an interesting visit. She just might get her wish after all, and Yasmine would come home for good this time.

Chapter 7

The cool air hit Holt's face and he turned up the lapels of the thick corduroy jacket he'd grabbed before making his way outside, following Yasmine.

He'd been aware of where she was at any given time throughout the entire party, and the moment he saw her make her escape out the front door, he was in hot pursuit.

And a pursuit was exactly what it was; he didn't try and tell himself otherwise. From the moment he'd picked her up from the airport, a growing fascination with her had begun, until now he had to find her. Had to find out…

Find out what?

Hell if he knew. But he wasn't going to pass up the opportunity to corner her, now that she was alone.

When Nate casually mentioned that Lilly was throwing an impromptu welcome-home party for Yasmine, he'd at first been tempted to give her warning, remembering the shy girl she'd been and unsure how she'd take such a welcome, no matter the good intentions behind it.

But the minute they'd called out "Surprise," he'd been taken aback by the ease with which she greeted everyone, grinning widely at the bevy of faces, many of whom she didn't know.

Throughout the party, although he'd given her space, allowing her to mingle without dogging her steps, he'd found himself smiling, drawn to her ringing laugh. And no matter where he was in the large room, or who he was talking to, he heard her laugh above the others, ringing out, drawing him in like a siren's call.

He noticed he wasn't alone in his attraction to her.

His foreman hadn't left her side for more than a few moments at a time since he'd seen her. Holt had no claims on her, he knew that. Hell, he hadn't seen her, not for any length of time, for over ten years.

But it didn't stop the anger from brewing and the need to stride across the room and knock his foreman as well as his best friend's teeth down his throat.

She'd made it through the crowded door, his eyes tracking her, when Jake had again found her. Holt nearly crushed the can of beer in his hand when Jake casually placed his arm around her waist.

He saw her smile and shake her head no, after several moments of conversation, before leaving the house. It was only then he released his death grip on the beer can.

Quickly he'd followed her after turning Sheila, the cousin of one of the older men, over to one of his men to keep her company. He ignored her pout, his mind solely on Yasmine as he'd left the house.

Now, as he scanned the porch and front yard, he didn't see her anywhere. He cursed, wondering where she could have gone, when he saw a small light on in the horses' shed near the house. Swiftly his stride ate up the distance, and once he reached the barn, he quietly opened the door and closed it tightly behind him.

"Oooh…you are a beautiful one. What's your name? Don't remember you here the last time I came home," he heard her voice croon softly.

He followed the sound of her voice and stopped when he came to Gerry's stall, the horse his brother Nate had recently purchased.

Casually he leaned against the door, watching her as she ran a hand over the horse's muzzle, issuing cooing sounds as she fed it a treat from the palm of her hand.

"You'd never know it, but just a couple of months ago you wouldn't have been able to get near that damn thing," he said, his voice breaking into the silence.

Yasmine spun around, her eyes widening when she saw him. "Oh God, you scared me to death," she said, her hand splayed over her chest.

He pushed away from the door and walked farther into the stall toward her. "I'm sorry. Didn't mean to frighten you. I saw you leave the party."

When he said nothing more, she raised a brow. "And?"

"And, I decided to follow you. Is that okay?" he asked, coming farther inside until he stood less than a foot away from her. He reached out a hand and ran it over the horse's silky mane. Holt felt her tension as soon as he stood near her. She glanced away, back to the horse, continuing to run her hand over it.

"Won't your girlfriend miss you?" Although her face was in profile, when she asked the question he saw the blush that stained her pretty brown skin.

"So...you did notice me," he murmured, stopping when he was less than a foot away from her. "I wasn't too sure of that. You seemed to have your fair amount of...attention," he replied.

She glanced his way and rolled her eyes, then turned back to the horse, slowly running her hands over its silky nuzzle. When it butted against her hand, she withdrew two more of the sugar cubes and fed them to the questing mouth. "Who wouldn't, with the way you two were carrying on?"

Holt laughed outright. "Carrying on? Surely that's a bit strong, Yas," he said, and purposely allowed his hand to brush against hers as she stroked the horse's muzzle.

He wasn't sure if he should be angry or pleased when she snatched her hand away as though his touch burned her.

She shrugged. "Nothing's changed, I see."

"Meaning?" She still kept her face in profile, but he saw the tightening of her jaw and frowned.

"Forget it." She shook her head, blowing out a breath. "Doesn't matter."

He stepped closer, placing two fingers beneath her chin, forcing her to look up at him.

"No. It does matter. You matter… Now, what did you mean?"

As he stared down into her upturned face, his frown intensified when he noted the way she quickly looked away from him, as though she couldn't stand to look at him.

"Yas…"

She brushed his hand away, forcing him to drop it at his side.

"Just forget it, Holt."

More curious than ever, instead of dropping it, he crowded her space even more, forcing her to look up at him.

Yasmine knew she should just shut up, just let him think whatever he wanted to think. But irritation with him was riding high. He was just too damn confident. No man should look as good as he did, have a voice that deep and sexy, and ooze sex with just a few chosen words.

She inhaled a deep breath. No man should smell like he did…

He stepped closer, crowding her space even more. She turned her head to the side, avoiding…him.

"Please…"

She felt his thumb beneath her chin, lifting it and forcing her to look up at him.

"You didn't answer my question, Yas," he murmured, his eyes trained directly on her lips.

Her tongue snaked out to lick her bottom rim.

"Meaning you're the same hotshot lover, the same guy who had time for every other girl but me. The same guy who…" She broke off, wanting to bite out her own tongue.

Damn him. Damn him for almost making her admit that he was the same man who had invaded her dreams in adolescence and hadn't let up since.

Yasmine was more than disgusted with herself. She thought she had it together. Thought she could handle coming home. Thought she could be the one to turn the tables on him.

She was a certified nutcase. She had to be, in thinking she could ever teach Holt a lesson, make him see her as anything other than what he always had—that little chubby girl she had been so long ago, crushin' on a boy who barely knew she existed.

She drew in a deep breath, the air caught at the back of her throat when she felt his long, lean fingers thumb her chin upward, forcing her to look at him.

She held the indrawn breath, her heart beating a harsh rhythm against her breast when she saw the look in his eyes… When she saw his head descend toward hers, her eyes fluttered closed.

The first touch of his lips against hers ignited a flame that blew Holt's earlier conviction that his fascination with her was a passing thing wide apart, like a pallet of dynamite.

He slanted his mouth over hers, taking nibbling bites from her plush lower rim, pulling it inside his mouth and laving it with his tongue. She whimpered when he released it, only to glide his tongue across the seam of her lips in a sensual seesawing motion until she parted them for him, silently inviting him inside.

When he felt her tentatively reach out and wrap her arms loosely around his neck, Holt brought her closer, flush against his body, her soft curves molding against his hard body, her big, beautiful breasts pressed tightly against him.

With a groan, he tunneled a hand beneath her hair, just below the low chignon she wore, dislodging the pins that held it in place. Her hair tumbled free and he sifted his fingers through the silky strands.

He placed his other hand around the small indenture of her waist, burrowing his fingers beneath the shirt she wore, until he felt the back clasp of her bra. Deftly, he unhooked the snaps.

Before she could let out a feeble protest, just as swiftly he unbuttoned her blouse, ripping one of the buttons from the opening in his haste.

The minute his fingers connected with her breasts, he growled low, deep in the back of his throat. He palmed the underside of the large orb in one hand, his thumb pressing over her tightening nipple.

With his other hand, his fingers dug deeper into her scalp, pressing her sweet mouth closer against his, eating her soft cries as he made his sensual assault against her mouth.

He was on fire for her. What had started out as a simple need to taste her, to find out if her lips were as soft as they looked, had escalated into a blazing need that was beginning to consume him.

And damned if he didn't want to get devoured in the blaze.

"God, you taste good, Yas." His voice was a raspy, sexy growl of need rumbling against the corner of her mouth. His hand was shaky as he caressed the generous mound he held cupped in his hand. "So damn good," he growled harshly, recapturing her mouth, dragging the upper swell deep inside his mouth before releasing it.

Yasmine's body went weak.

"So do you, Holt," she softly moaned. Even to her own ears, her voice sounded foreign, thready with the need that was running so high she could barely speak.

When his tongue snaked out and trailed a hot, scorching path from the corner of her mouth to the lobe of her ear, she arched her back, pressing herself into his hardness, her body on fire with need. Had he not held her so close, so tight against his body, she would have tumbled straight onto the floor.

"Touch me," he rasped. He yanked at several of his buttons, ripping his shirt open before taking one of her hands from where it rested around his neck and placing it over his hard chest.

She closed her eyes, her breath coming out in strangled gasps.

Hesitantly at first, she feathered her hand over his chest. Daringly, she fingered one of his small male nipples, watching in fascination as it beaded against her fingers.

When she heard him groan, she glanced up at him. The gleam from the moon lit the shed, casting his handsome face in a sensual, harsh glow. He brought her fingers up to his mouth, opening her palm and placing a kiss in the center.

When he opened his eyes and looked down at her, the look of lust and need stamped harshly on his handsome face, she drew in a deep breath.

"I need you."

With that, Yasmine's heart, already beating out of control, nearly leaped from her chest.

She stared at him, reading the lust, the need and desire blazing from his bright blue gaze.

God, she'd wanted this man for her entire life, it seemed. For him to ask her…beg her, to make love to her, was something straight out of one of her fantasies.

She placed her hand over his cheek, feeling the stubble roughly caress her palm.

"Holt, I—"

"Holt, I know you're in here, come out, come out, wherever you are," a singsong voice called out, interrupting Yasmine before she could continue.

Chapter 8

"All settled in, sweetheart?"

Yasmine yawned hugely as she entered the kitchen, glancing over at her aunt. She could only see the back of her head, as her back was to Yasmine, her aunt's arm reaching overhead in the process of removing a pot from its position hanging above the stove.

"I still have to unpack, but I'll save that for later," she said, before looking around the large, open kitchen, the blinds opened, allowing the sun to flood the airy room.

She'd always loved this kitchen, and it was the one room in the house that had remained nearly untouched, looking much as it had when she'd called the ranch home.

The kitchen had been updated with modern conveniences, yet it maintained an old-world charm. White slatted blinds covered each of the six large windows that gave the room its natural light. Terra-cotta tiles on the floor and white wood cabinets gave the room a homey ambience.

She grimaced. The minute she yawned, the pounding in her head increased tenfold.

Not only did she have a headache the size of the Teton Mountains, her eyes had been so swollen she'd barely been able to pry them open that morning, her mouth was dry as sandpaper…and she was in *desperate* need of mass quantities of caffeine.

"Got any coffee, Aunt Lilly?" she asked, shuffling toward one of the high-backed stools surrounding the marble counter.

Lord only knew if she could open a vein and directly infuse caffeine into her system she would. Right now she'd do just about anything to stop the little man in her head from his relentless drumming.

God, what a night.

Piggybacking that thought, images of her and Holt, what they done…what they'd *almost* done, flooded her mind, and she covered her eyes with her hands, as though that would make the images disappear from her mind.

She'd been moments away from giving in to something she'd fantasized about for over ten years. She'd been moments away from giving in to what his eyes, his mouth…his very touch promised he wanted to deliver. And had they not been interrupted she would have done just that. Given in to everything his carnal gaze was promising and more.

After leaving the shed last night, Yasmine had fled back to the house and found her aunt, telling her she was tired from the day's travel and was ready to go to bed. It had taken a fair amount of willpower not to rush to her room in order to avoid Lilly, fearing she'd read in her eyes her embarrassment and guess who was the reason.

When her aunt had seemed oblivious to her state of turmoil, Yasmine had sighed in relief, and after bidding a quick goodbye to as many people as she could, she'd been seconds away from fleeing to the sanctity of her room when her aunt's voice stopped her.

"Before you go, Yasmine, did something...or someone, upset you?" Lilly had asked bluntly, a frown marring her otherwise unlined face.

She caught Lilly looking around, and when her eyes narrowed, Yasmine had turned in the direction she was staring and saw Holt walking through the front door, his eyes scanning the crowd.

"Oh, God, no! I mean, it's nothing, Auntie. Nothing happened," she said, desperate to get away. "We, uh, talked, that's all. Really, it's nothing. I'm just tired. It's been a long day, and I still haven't unpacked."

"Would have thought you all had done enough talking on the ride home," she said. Yasmine was seconds away from completely losing it, battling back the ridiculous tears hovering.

Finally, after one last speculative look, her aunt

sighed, gave Yasmine a swift hug and asked if she needed help unpacking. Yasmine had managed to refrain from screaming out a no, she was so desperate to go to her room, already reliving the last few moments when she and Holt had been interrupted in the shed.

Not only had they been interrupted—Holt with his shirt open, hair disheveled, and she with her blouse on the floor, her bra dangling off her shoulders—but they'd been interrupted by the woman who'd been by Holt's side the entire night, a woman Yasmine could only assume was his current girlfriend.

They'd both heard the woman's call, and had just enough time to re-dress before she found them.

Embarrassed, Yasmine had fled, evading Holt's outstretched hands and demands for her to remain where she was. She ran past the woman, barely cataloging her narrowed eyes as her gaze collided with hers for a brief moment.

It hadn't helped matters in the least when, after taking her shower and wanting nothing more than to jump into bed, she'd checked her cell and seen that she'd missed four calls, and all had been from Clayton Moore.

"Oh, God…" she'd moaned, flopping back on the bed and clicking the icon that took her to her voice mail.

Men like Clayton, rich, handsome, sophisticated, could have their choice of women. Although she had no interest in him outside of business, she would be lying if she said his interest hadn't been flattering.

Not that she didn't think she was worthy of a man like Clayton having a personal interest in her. She had a mirror and was as aware of her attributes, physical and intellectual, as well as her flaws. She could, and had, attracted men of all types.

But with everything combined, winning the competition, the offer of her own show on the food channel as well Clayton's offer…although it had all seemed surreal, at the same time it had been overwhelming. Which was why the call from her aunt had been a mixed bag of blessings for her.

She knew she needed the time to sort everything out, her life, both professional and personal.

When she'd listened to his deep voice on her voice mail—*and when did he develop that slightly nasal tone in his voice?* Yasmine thought, expecting the slightly giddy feeling she'd gotten the previous times she'd heard his voice she was chagrined to feel absolutely nothing. Nada. Zip.

After listening to the call, she'd sat on the edge of the bed, completely befuddled…and irritated.

Damn him.

It was all Holt's fault, she'd thought in irritation. Everything had been running smoothly, her life couldn't have been going any better, and he had to come back into her life. He had to kiss her and renew that silly girlhood crush, one she had been determined to put behind her once and for all.

He had to look at her with those smoldering blue eyes of his…Stetson low, deep baritone washing over her body, giving her goose bumps in places that made her blush to the bone.

She could still feel the imprint of his callused palms as they brushed across her nipples.

Yasmine inhaled a deep breath, catching the bottom rim of her lip between her teeth.

One hand hesitantly moved up the nightshirt she wore, past her stomach, to lightly cup one of her breasts.

Just as hesitantly a finger brushed over her nipple. Pinching it, she rolled the tightening nub between two fingers. The other hand ran down her thigh and touched her mound.

She felt her breath coming faster.

When her cell rang again, startling her, her eyes sprang open. She glanced around as though someone had caught her, feeling the heat across her cheeks.

Fumbling, she'd reached for her cell, punching the button and rasping out a hello.

When she heard Clayton's voice on the other end, she forced aside the disappointment that his voice wasn't the one she wanted to hear and tried to inject as much enthusiasm into her voice as she could.

She broke into his monologue, telling him as gently as she could that she was tired and really just wanted to go to bed; that she'd speak to him as soon as she'd gotten some rest and would call the next day.

He must have noticed something was wrong. There had been a distinct chill in his voice when he'd said goodbye, telling her that if she didn't reach him to just leave a message with his assistant and he'd get back to her as soon as possible.

So much for having more than a professional interest

in her, she thought, raising a brow at the phone when the silence on the other end told her that he'd hung up.

If his offer was solid, then it would be there when she was ready to make the decision, she'd thought. No one was going to push or press her into doing anything she wasn't sure of.

After that she'd pulled back the sheets, and the minute her head had hit the pillow, she slept like the dead, the clichéd rooster call waking her up the next morning.

Now Yasmine glanced at her aunt, frowning deeply when she noticed the way she was favoring her right leg as she made her way to the sink, a large pot held in her hand.

Immediately Yasmine felt horrible. Here she was selfishly thinking of her own issues, and her aunt was in pain.

She jumped up, nearly upsetting her chair. Righting it, she swiftly made her way over to her aunt, taking the large pot away from her.

"Now, baby, I can do that! Yas…"

"Go sit down, Aunt Lilly! I've got this… Just point and direct. That's what I'm here for. To help you. That's the only reason I'm here," she said, reminding herself as much as she was her aunt. With a shooing motion, she forced her aunt to move away.

"Fine, I know when I'm not needed," Lilly harrumphed, but Yasmine saw the relieved look in her dark eyes before she limped over to the table in the kitchen and sat down. "Oh, shoot, forgot my tea," she said, pushing her hands on the table, preparing to rise,

To Love a Wilde

when Yasmine shot her a look. "I swear, Aunt Lilly, if you get back up again…" She allowed the threat to dangle, and laughed at the look that crossed her aunt's face.

Her aunt placed her hands up, palms out, in silent surrender. "Fine. But I don't want to get used to all of this catering. What am I going to do when you leave me all alone and I have to go back to flying solo?"

"Flying solo?" she asked, frowning at her aunt as she filled the large pot with water.

After her aunt nodded toward the vegetables on one of the side tables, Yasmine absently grabbed a cutting knife from the large butcher block and made short work of chopping the veggies before adding them to the pot.

She heard her aunt sigh. "No, now don't get me wrong, the boys always make sure I have plenty of help. I guess I just sometimes really miss you, Yas. Nothing like having another woman in the house. Sometimes there's too much darn testosterone flying around here for my peace of mind. Works my third nerve sometimes, when all I have is two to spare," she said, and both women laughed.

After the laughter died down, Yasmine asked, "What about Althea? She seems pretty nice. Does she help you out at all?" She frowned, realizing she didn't know much about Althea. "Or does she have her own career?"

"Oh, she is, baby. She's a really sweet girl. Been through a lot, too. Yes, she helps me a lot. Right now she's so busy with planning the wedding that I hate to bother her. Besides, I guess I just miss you a whole lot, Yas, that's all."

Yasmine added the meat her aunt had already cut into medallions into the pot. She shifted through the spices on the rack, mentally taking note of the missing spices she would buy when she went to town, as she contemplated her aunt's last words.

"I miss you, too, Aunt Lilly…it's just—" She started before her aunt stopped her.

"I know. You have your life. And I'm proud of you, I really am. I just wish…" She paused and continued, "I wish you would come out to visit more, Yas. That's all."

Yasmine sighed. She knew her aunt was proud of her, knew she wanted the best for her. She also knew that her aunt missed her and would love nothing more than for Yasmine to come home more often—she'd never made any secret of that fact. However, left unsaid between the two of them was the reason that would never happen.

Her aunt was well aware of what made her visits to the ranch few and far between: Holt Wilde.

Although they'd never openly discussed it, Yasmine being too embarrassed to open up to her aunt about her adolescent fascination with him, her aunt still knew.

"But maybe…maybe I can come out here to visit more often, Aunt Lilly," she said, and knew she'd said the right thing when her aunt smiled, nodding her head.

"That would be a start," she quipped, and Yasmine raised a brow.

"A start?"

"For now," she said mysteriously, and Yasmine shook her head. She didn't think she wanted to know what was behind the little smile on her aunt's face.

As Lilly played with the spoon in her cup, stirring the contents of the herbal tea she favored with absentminded attention, Yasmine busied herself with the preparations for the noontime meal.

"Yasmine, about last night…"

"Good morning, Miss Lilly," a cheery voice interrupted before her aunt could finish her thought.

"Good morning, Althea," she said, smiling over at the woman.

"Oh, hi, Yasmine, I didn't see you there!" Althea Hudson, Nate's fiancée, said as she walked over to where Lilly sat. She planted a loud, smacking kiss on her aunt's cheek.

Although Lilly made a shooing motion with her hand, Yasmine saw that she enjoyed the affectionate kiss.

It was good to know that her aunt had another female at the ranch; since Yasmine left, Lilly had been the only one. And after meeting Althea yesterday, she was already beginning to like her and was glad to know she'd be around for her aunt when she left again.

When Althea glanced her way, she smiled. "I came in to see if you needed any help, Miss Lilly, before Nate and I have to visit the pastor this afternoon for our premarital counseling." She paused, looking at Yasmine, a hesitant look on her face. "Looks like Yas beat me to it."

Yasmine pushed away the momentary sting of jealousy and motioned Althea over. "Girl, come on over here, there is more than enough for you to do!"

Yasmine grinned back at her when Althea's smile returned as she donned an apron, joining her at the counter.

"Now, as your aunt will tell you, although I'm not exactly the world's *greatest* cook, I know my way around the kitchen a bit," she said, a smug look on her face. "I think I can hold my own."

"Oh, Lord," Yasmine heard her aunt mutter, hearing the underlying humor in her voice.

Yasmine raised a brow and turned to look up at Althea, as she was several inches taller than she. "Oh, can you now? Oh, okay…cool! How about you help me make a special dish for the men. Nothing too fancy, just something to thank them for helping with my party. Let's see here," she said, pretending she was really thinking hard about what she wanted to place on the menu. She snapped her fingers. "Got it! I was thinking about starting with a *crêpe au fromage de chèvre,* as an appetizer. I think Aunt Lilly has some fresh spinach, I can go into town for the rest." She frowned again, "Maybe top it off with a *poulet aux porto*…I know for sure I saw some chicken breasts in the freezer…and for desert something simple like crêpes suzettes. What do you think?" she asked, biting the inside of her cheek to stop the grin from breaking free when she saw the way Althea's eyes widened in alarm.

"Uhhh…I was thinking more along the lines of

peeling potatoes?" she said, ending the statement as a question, and both women laughed.

"Girl, if I presented the guys with that menu, they'd look at me like I was crazy," she said. "So, yes, I can definitely use help peeling the veggies… These are 'steak and potatoes' type of guys, all the way!"

"I think you two might need me after all," Lilly said, laughing along with them. "I can't let the two of you have all the fun without me!" When she tried to get up, both women turned toward her, simultaneously issuing the order for her to "sit!"

With a resigned look Lilly sat back down, but before she turned away, Yasmine saw the pleased look cross her face and felt an answering happiness bubble up inside her. It had been a long time since she'd felt any type of female camaraderie. Too long.

In fact, the only times in her life when she had had been when she was with her aunt, the two of them usually in the kitchen, discussing everything from life to arguing about which was the best way to cook a roast. Maybe, despite the oddness and all-around craziness that her life had suddenly become, her visit might be the best thing that had happened to her in a long time.

She hoped it would be. It was time to lay to rest old ghosts and decide which direction to take in her career as well as her private life.

Chapter 9

"Have you given it any more thought?"

"What about? Catering the wedding? Yes, I told you I would love to!"

"No. I mean, yes, about the wedding, but also about you opening a business. I was talking about it with Nate. He agreed it would be a fantastic idea. There isn't anyone nearby who is doing anything like that, you'd have an open field, could provide something that is sorely lacking."

Holt paused, stopping dead in his tracks as he had been headed toward the kitchen.

He frowned. He hadn't known Yasmine had been thinking of starting a catering business. But why that should surprise him he had no idea. She was definitely a woman of purpose.

It had been nearly a week since his encounter with Yasmine in the horse stable. A week of her avoiding him. A week of remembering their explosive kiss in the barn. A week of thinking of her, nonstop.

With both of them living in the house, it had made it difficult for her to avoid him completely, but she'd managed to not be in the same room with him alone at any given time.

Not that he'd made it easy for her. He felt like a damn fool with the amount of times he'd made excuses to head back to the house, particularly with it being one of their busiest seasons, moving herd and getting ready for calving season as well as marketing the cattle.

After he'd gotten rid of Sheila after her ill-timed interruption of his and Yasmine's scalding encounter, Holt had rushed inside the house in search of her, only to find she was no longer at her own welcome-home party.

Frustrated, he'd found one of his brothers and asked if he knew where Yasmine had gone, trying to be as casual as possible. It was then that Lilly had walked up behind him and informed him in a voice gone ice-cold that Yasmine had decided to call it a night. Although she'd been succinct, not giving more details besides the bare essential, her stony expression spoke volumes. She might not have known what happened, but he'd bet his prize steer on the fact that she thought he had something to do with it.

Tempted to badger Lilly for more info, Holt had glanced toward his brother Nate, who stood near his bride-to-be, Althea, and caught the subtle shake of his head, telling him to leave it alone.

No one could ever accuse Holt of being the type to scare easily, but when it came to Miss Lilly…well, a man knew when to hold his cards and when to fold them and walk away. For now, he walked away.

He'd spent the rest of the evening evading his brothers, after realizing they suspected something was up, not wanting to deal with their questions. He'd had more than his fill trying to figure out what in hell he had to do to fix the mess he'd created, without dealing with his nosy brothers, as well.

The next morning he'd woken with a pounding headache…with his hand fisting his shaft, rock hard, from a night spent having the type of wet dreams that would make a prepubescent boy blush.

And the rest of the week hadn't been any different.

Night after night his dreams got more and more erotic, the two of them doing things together that if Lilly even suspected he was thinking of doing to her beloved niece, she'd run him off his own ranch.

Yesterday he'd spent the majority of the day fighting the urge to find her, trying to get her out of his mind for all the good it had done him. After tending to the early-morning jobs on the south section of the ranch, he'd cut out early, leaving the rest of the work to his men, ready to find Yasmine. But he soon realized she was just as intent on keeping her distance from him as he was on trying to get to her

Last night, after coming in late from helping the

vet with two births, he'd come up the stairs and been surprised she was still up. Thinking he'd finally get some time with her alone, he'd began to walk toward her, only for her to take one look at him and spin around and slam the door to her room in his face, leaving him to wonder what in hell he'd done that time to anger her so.

When he'd learned that Jake was going to take Yasmine and Miss Lilly to Sheridan to the Memorial Hospital for her surgery, he'd informed his brothers he'd be the one to take them instead. She wouldn't be able to avoid him then.

He wasn't sure who it surprised more, him or his brothers, his volunteering. But there was no way in hell he was going to allow Jake to do it, after the way he all but rolled over and asked her to rub his stomach as he catered to her at the party like a well-trained dog.

Although they hadn't asked or protested his decision, he rushed in to explain that Jake was scheduled to accompany Nate to Cheyenne for an upcoming auction.

"Can you guys do without me for a few days?" he'd asked, as the plan was to stay for the three days it would take for the surgery and her recovery before driving back home.

"Holt, man, you don't have to give us a reason. And, yeah, of course we can handle it—we have enough men to cover. You take care of Lilly and Yas, we'll take care of the ranch," Nate had broken in drily when Holt continued to rationalize his reasons. Holt caught the look he and Shilah shared. "I'm sure Yas will appreciate the gesture."

Holt hadn't been so sure of that with the way she'd avoided him like the plague the past week. But she wouldn't be able to avoid him when he drove her and Lilly to the hospital. The four-hour drive was a guarantee that she wouldn't.

When the others broke for lunch, Holt had forgone eating and instead gone to the house, on the pretense of finding Lilly to discuss her upcoming operation. Now, he continued to listen to Althea and Yasmine.

"I know Miss Lilly would love to have you come back home," Althea said, quietly.

"Please don't tell me you talked about that with Aunt Lilly?" was Yasmine's response

"Oh, goodness, no," Althea laughed. "I wouldn't do that to you," she finished, and he heard Yasmine's relieved laughter.

"If she even thought for a minute…"

"I know." There was a pause. "No, I wouldn't dare say anything."

"Good." There was another pause and Holt leaned closer, straining to hear.

It was long moments before Yasmine continued, her tone nonchalant. "Besides, we're only talking about me catering your wedding. As far as me opening a business…before I could even give that any serious thought…which I haven't—" he heard her say, her tone cautious "—but before I even gave it any serious consideration, if I were to do that, I'd have to talk to the brothers about it."

Immediately Althea responded. "I don't think you'd have any worries on that score. They all love you, Yasmine. They'd love to have you back home."

There was a long pause and Holt became even more still, waiting to hear Yasmine's response.

"Especially Holt."

At Althea's remark, his frown increased. Was it that obvious how interested he was in her?

"Oh, I don't think it would matter to Holt one way or another," she said, her voice light. It was long moments before she continued, her voice so casual, so nonchalant, had he not known her better, he would think she was brushing it off as nothing. But beneath the tone he heard a subtle nervousness to the laughter.

"Well, you've got a lot of options, Yasmine. That's just one. I wanted you to know that although we've only just met, I would also like it if you gave it some thought. Coming home, starting your business. I would help in any way I could. We haven't known each other long… but, well, you're like the sister I've never had. I would help you in any way I could. As long as you don't mind it being the grunt work." She laughed. "My cooking skills are nowhere up to par with yours." Holt heard the rustle of clothing and knew the two women had embraced.

"Thank you, Althea. That means a lot."

He heard movement and quickly moved out of the line of vision before either one of the women knew he was there.

He wondered when, over the past few days, Yasmine had begun to think about opening a catering business and returning home.

He hadn't heard about it from either of his brothers. From the conversation, obviously Nate knew of her plans. He wondered if Shilah knew as well, and if so, why he was left in the dark. He understood not telling Lilly, not wanting to build her expectations unless the plans were finalized, but why not tell him?

Holt waited until he heard Althea leave before making his presence known. Walking farther into the kitchen he stood watching Yasmine. From his field of vision he had a nice visual of her shapely behind, cupped sweetly in the skirt she wore as she bent over the stove.

A short-sleeved white blouse was tucked neatly into the waistband, and the ends of her apron tied in a bow near the top of her butt made him want to unwrap the pretty package she presented.

On her feet, again, she wore heels; although not as high as the ones she'd worn the day he'd picked her up from the airport, they still added definition to her already shapely legs.

She withdrew a large pan of what looked like muffins from the oven and stood back.

"I think my babies are too pretty to eat," she said, and laughed lightly, dusting her hands down the sides of her apron as she admired her creation.

"I think I have to disagree with that," he said as he admired her shapely backside.

"I—I didn't see you there. When did you get here?" she said, spinning around to face him.

He ran a gaze over her body, past her small feet in the dainty little heels, past the short skirt that hugged her curvy hips to sinful perfection to the pulse banging at the hollow of her throat, before meeting her eyes.

Yes, she was definitely a sweet morsel he'd love to sink his teeth into. He grinned, walking farther into the room.

Thinking she was alone, Yasmine's heart leaped wildly against her chest when she heard the deep baritone voice speak behind her.

As Holt sauntered toward her, his insolent stare roaming over her body, she cast a nervous glance around, realizing she was alone with him.

So, her day of reckoning had come. She'd wondered how long it would be before he'd catch her alone. She'd fooled herself into thinking he'd given up.

Late last night, restless, thinking of the many decisions facing her, she'd finally given up on sleep. Glancing at her cell phone she saw that she'd missed Clayton's call.

That made the third one in as many days. She knew her mind should be on her career. It should be, but it wasn't. Every time she sat down and turned to her spreadsheet with the pros and cons of each career move, a method she'd used to organize her thoughts since college days, she'd find her mind wandering, thoughts of Holt invading her mind with irritating precision.

Thinking a good bath would relax her enough so she could get some rest, she'd grabbed her toiletry bag and walked down the hallway to the bathroom.

Although fully modernized, with private baths included in the four master suites the men had added, the room she'd been given didn't have that luxury.

When she'd spoken to Lilly after agreeing to come home, she'd assured her aunt that her old room would be fine for her to stay in. And she was glad she had.

As she'd sunk down into the claw-foot tub, hoping the Epsom salts and warm water would do their job, she'd forced everything from her mind, everything that had been crowding, taking up space, and simply relaxed. She thought of the memories associated with the room she occupied, reminding her of her time growing up at the ranch. She cherished them all. Coming to the ranch after the death of her parents, she remembered how sad, afraid and alone she'd felt. More important, she remembered how welcome everyone at Wyoming Wilde had made her feel. How they'd made her feel as if she was a part of the family.

The bath *had* done the job, and Yasmine felt relaxed enough to hopefully get some sleep. Gathering her clothes, she'd left the room. As it was past midnight she'd come out of the bathroom with nothing more than a towel wrapped around her body. Looking up and down the hallway, she'd seen the coast was clear and had made a mad dash for her room.

Just as she'd made it to her door, she'd *felt* his presence.

Pausing with her hand on the doorknob, she'd slowly turned around. He stood poised at the entry to his own door, several feet down the hallway, staring at her.

Although the roles were reversed, as she was the one wearing the towel, Yasmine felt an odd sense of déjà vu.

His eyes dropped from hers and casually raked over her towel-clad body. Although all her major essentials were covered, she felt naked, exposed beneath his hot stare.

Forcing herself to break away, her gaze slid over him, as well. She took in the jeans, dirty from work, and shirt, dampened with sweat that clung to his chest, before her glance fell to his hat, held in his hand.

His hat was in his hand.

It was well past midnight, and everyone had returned home hours before.

Her jaw tightened.

Like the tomcat he was, he had just dragged himself home.

"Yasmine. I'm glad you're up. I think we need to talk," he'd begun, walking toward her.

Breaking the spell he seemed to cast on her with the ease of a seasoned wizard, she didn't dignify him with an answer.

Instead she spun around and opened the door to her room. She heard his muttered curse behind her as she slammed the door shut behind her, in his face. And added insult to injury by turning the key in the lock.

She watched him now as he moved farther into the

kitchen, his mere presence crowding her space and making her feel strangely claustrophobic. He was just too big, too…everything, for her peace of mind.

He drew in a deep breath. "Smells good in here. What are you cooking?" he asked, casually lifting the lids of several of the large pots she had on the stove.

"Finishing up the noontime lunch for the men," she said, turning away from him and busying herself at the stove.

"Where's Lilly?"

"In her room, resting," she said, leaning down to pull out the warming dishes. "She was limping again, although she tried to hide it from me. So I made her go and rest and told her that I would take care of lunch," she said, her voice muffled.

"That couldn't have been an easy thing to do." He laughed, leaning against a nearby pillar.

"No, it wasn't. Took a fair amount of reasoning," Yasmine said, rising and casting a look his way. She frowned when she caught his eyes glued to her back end. Purposely putting more sway to her walk than was necessary, she strolled over to the center aisle and laid the trays down.

"And by reasoning I'm assuming you mean bullying?" Although he continued the thread of the conversation, he didn't even have the decency to *pretend* as though he wasn't eyeing her butt.

Tomcat was too mild a name for Holt Wilde.

A few more apt, choice names came to mind, ones she

knew would make her aunt go old-school and wash her mouth out if she knew what Yasmine was thinking.

"Yeah, there was a lot of that, too," Yasmine replied. "She can be obstinate, particularly when it comes to her kitchen."

"I'm sure you're more than woman enough and up for the challenge. Even for Miss Lilly," he replied.

Yasmine decided to ignore his not-so-subtle flirting.

"It's her domain. I can respect that," she answered with a shrug. "Before she allowed me to work it alone, she gave me a list of things to do." Yasmine nodded a head toward the sheet of paper on the counter with a laugh. "Along with a laundry list of other do's and don'ts—" she shook her head, her smile fixed in place "—but her surgery is coming up in a few days. She finally caved. I think she knows as well that she needs to rest as much as possible. Besides, I've got everything under control." She finished transferring the food from the pots into the warming pans, watching him from beneath lowered lids as he casually lifted the various lids, inhaling the aromatic scent that wafted from the steaming contents, a blissful look on his face.

Although it was barely noon, his hair was already plastered to his well-shaped head, dampened from working. The sleeves of his blue chambray work shirt were rolled up, exposing thick forearms lightly covered in a dusting of hair. The jeans he wore were old and faded, and like all the others, he wore cowboy boots, scuffed, old.

Nothing special.

But why did he look so good to her that Yasmine felt the walls of her femininity contract and release, the response one that was purely physical, feminine and out of her control. She inhaled, and even though he stood away from her, she could smell him.

His unique scent blew across her nose, overpowering the food she'd spent most of the morning preparing.

She drew in an involuntary breath. As much as she wanted to deny it, his mere presence was like an aphrodisiac, drawing her in. Intoxicating.

This was crazy, this hold he seemed to have on her, one that made being in the same room with him make her feel like a cat in heat. The more she was around him, the more the attraction seemed to grow. It didn't matter if he was physically around her or not, as she'd not been able to go more than a few minutes without thinking about him.

When she lifted the last pot to transfer it, he took it from her hands, finishing the tasks for her. "Let me do that. Isn't Lilly supposed to have someone in here, helping? I thought Nate hired someone from town."

Yasmine stood back, allowing him to finish the task, admiring the way his muscles lightly bunched and flexed as he effortlessly handled the heavy pots.

"He did. Usually he comes in around this time to help out. I'm not sure what happened to this one. Aunt Lilly says when she gets back she's taking over hiring someone to help out. The ones Nate picks never seem to work out."

After he finished he turned to her. "Well, until she does, consider me your sous-chef," he said, bowing at the waist. "Your wish is my command."

Yasmine tried not to allow his charming banter, something that came as easy to him as breathing was to other men, to affect her.

She tried.

But it didn't do much good. The ends of her mouth quirked up in a grin she tried to suppress.

"What? Did I use the wrong term?" he asked, frowning. "I'm just a dumb cowboy. I don't know much about you city folks and your highbrow way of life."

"Oh, whatever." She laughed outright. "Don't even try it with me, Holt *Magnum* Wilde!" she quipped, knowing how much he disliked his middle name. "I happen to know that not only did you get your bachelor's degree but that you also managed to finish your master's while playing for the NFL," she finished smugly, and immediately wanted to bite out her own tongue.

He slowly advanced on her, the sexy grin on his face widening. "So…you've been keeping tabs on me Yasmine *Nicole* Taylor." It was a statement more than a question. Tit for tat.

"No more so than you have of me," she volleyed back.

His lips quirked sexily, the small dimple near the corner of his mouth deepening.

"Touché," he said, laughing. "Guilty as charged." He shrugged his big shoulders. He'd been steadily advancing on her. The closer he got, the more she retreated, until she came to a stop when her back brushed up against the refrigerator door.

He stopped in front of her, his body close to hers. He ran his finger softly down the side of her face, a strange look on his. "That I have. What can I say? You've got me fascinated. You have for a long time."

"And why is that?" She looked up at him. "Nothing about me is all that interesting. Nothing like the women you're used to…being around."

Just as quickly as their banter began, it ended, the energy between them becoming charged with a subtle sensuality that was as sudden as it was intense.

She swallowed and turned away from his intent stare.

When she would have moved out of reach, both of his arms came out to bracket her body, effectively caging her in.

"None of them can hold a candle to you, Yas," he said, his voice low, forcing her to look at him by placing a finger beneath her chin.

Yasmine drew in a deep breath. As she looked up into his eyes, images of the kiss they shared, the way he'd wrapped her in his big arms, made goose bumps break out over her exposed arms.

He drew closer to her, wrapping an arm around her waist and smoothly pulling her body closer to his. Unable to move, she stood within his embrace, waiting.

"Why did you run from me, Yas?" he asked.

His question was like ice water being dumped over

her head, dragging her out of the sensual web he'd created.

She placed her hands against his chest and shoved. Catching him off guard, she pushed away from him.

"What is it, Holt? One woman not enough for you? Don't you get tired of playing the role?" Yasmine spun and faced him.

"What role?" he asked, a puzzled look on his face. "What are you talking about?"

Yasmine felt resurging anger as she thought of the woman who'd interrupted them that night in the shed, as well as the after-midnight…booty call…she'd caught him returning from last night. It was probably the same woman.

Or maybe not. Her lips curled. "Penthouse," as he'd been called, had a reputation for having several women at his beck and call at any given notice.

"The whole Casanova thing. Remember your girlfriend? The one from Saturday? What was her name?" she asked, frowning. "Was she the same one you came home from last night? Maybe it was a different one. I heard one is never enough for *Penthouse,*" she said, drawling out the nickname.

"Don't call me that," he bit out, his features pinched, his jaw tightening in anger.

"Why, Holt? Truth hurts?"

The anger dropped from his face, replaced by a grin. Warily she eyed him.

"You're jealous."

"Not even on your best day," she replied, narrowing

her eyes. "And that little look of yours?" She shook her head. "That is *so* not working for me."

He moved closer again, oblivious to her feigned nonchalance. "What look? The look of a man who knows what he wants?"

When she found herself in the same spot she'd been in moments before, backed up against the refrigerator, him closing in on her, she raised a hand. As though that would make him stop.

"No, the look of a tomcat on the prowl."

Her words had no effect on him this time, nor did her resistance. If anything, they made him bolder.

She swallowed, forcing herself to stand her ground, refusing to show him just how much his words affected her.

He didn't stop until their bodies brushed against each other, her breasts pressed intimately against the top of his stomach.

He brought his finger beneath her chin, forcing her to look at him. "No, baby," he said, his voice low, his bright blue eyes gleaming. "That's not what this look is. This is the look of a man who knows what he wants."

Everything grew still, including the very air around them. She saw his eyes run over her face until they focused on her lips.

She opened her mouth to give a swift rebuttal but promptly shut it.

Both her mouth and lips felt like cotton, they were so dry. She ran a tongue over them, and before she realized his intent, he swooped down and captured her tongue between his teeth.

She moaned, all of her righteous anger going up in smoke the minute their mouths met.

He cupped the back of her head, aligning their mouths with one hand. The other he used to cup her bottom, bringing her tightly against him, and Yasmine sank into the kiss.

Gently, as though not to scare her, he pried her mouth open and pressed his tongue deep inside. His mouth was hard yet yielding, soft yet firm. Perfect.

After long moments when he simply kissed her, he released her mouth to rain kisses down the line of her throat, his wicked tongue lapping between the seam of her breasts, and Yasmine cried out softly.

Retracing his path, his tongue flickered out to dart and caress its way back, until he reached the corner of her mouth.

"So sweet," he murmured, before stroking his tongue over the seam of her mouth.

On fire, hungry for his tongue, his mouth, his touch, Yasmine rose on tiptoes and wrapped her arms around his neck to pull him closer.

His hand moved from the back of her neck, his roughened, callused palms sliding over the skin of her throat, making her body arch sharply, before cupping one of her breasts. She sighed into his mouth when he ran his thumb over her nipple.

Beneath her bra she felt her nipple grow erect, pushing insistently against the fabric.

"Holt," she whispered against his mouth. "Please…" She stopped when two fingers pinched the nipple, the sensation sharp but not unpleasant.

"God, your mouth is sweet," he growled. "I can't get enough of it." He pushed away from her, his breath harsh as he ran a hand through his hair and ran an eye over her disheveled body. "I can't get enough of you—" the admission was dragged from him "—I haven't been able to get you out of my mind since Saturday," he said.

He captured her mouth, dragged her body closer and lavished his attention on her. Licking and suckling her lips, he ate at her mouth as though it was food from the gods.

Yasmine squirmed, her body caught between the hard door of the refrigerator and the even harder wall of his chest.

In her movement, her elbow hit the ice lever of the refrigerator, and seconds later ice ran down her back.

Yelping, she pushed away from Holt and the refrigerator.

"What?" He breathed the word, his breaths coming out harshly.

"Ice…down my back," she hissed.

She glanced up at him, seeing the sensuality still stamped on his features.

When he moved to draw her nearer, she held up a staying hand, shaking her head no.

The ice had been just what the doctor ordered, forcing her to pull up and decloud her murky vision.

"Stop right there." She drew in a deep, fortifying

breath. "You need to go." It took all she had to push him away.

"Yasmine, what's wrong?" He frowned, moving toward her as she backpedaled away, both physically and mentally.

"This…whatever we have going on between us, needs to end. I don't need this." She waved her hands in the air. "You…whatever, in my life. My life is complicated enough."

"Is that what I am to you? A complication?"

His jaw hardened and the corner of his mouth twitched.

"Yes. That's *all* you are. And I've got other things to think about," she said, and could tell her response angered him more.

"Well, while you're deciding what you want, think about this," he said. He reached out, grabbed her by the waist and hauled her close. Her breath escaped on a startled rush of air when he slammed his mouth over hers.

The kiss was short but no less hot.

As soon as it began, it was over, and Yasmine stumbled a bit when he moved away from her, her legs like jelly. She righted herself against the counter and watched as he turned on his boot heel and left without another word. The minute she was alone, her body slumped.

Slowly she moved away and went to the oven. With shaky hands she dumped the cooled muffins into plastic containers, her mind whirling. She'd done everything in her power to avoid him over the past few days, which hadn't been easy, living in the same house, keeping her hands and mind busy. As her aunt said, an idle mind was the devil's playground.

She was finding that for her the devil was all wrapped up in perfect masculinity by the name of Holt Wilde.

Chapter 10

Business returned to usual the day following Yasmine's encounter with Holt.

She also managed to avoid Holt as much as possible. She'd learned the men's schedule from Lilly and Althea. Nate was the first of the brothers to come home, usually to see his wife. With their upcoming preparations for the wedding, the two of them usually took to the study and would eat a later dinner, together.

As soon as Nate arrived, Yasmine would quickly finish her work, eat with Lilly and retire to her room. Their last encounter still lay heavy on her mind. Although she didn't want him thinking it meant any more to her than it had him, she'd be lying if she tried to convince herself of that fact.

Or that it didn't matter to her that he no longer tried

to seek her out, dogging her footsteps as he had before in an attempt to pick up where they'd left off.

Yasmine convinced herself that that only served as a relief. She completely ignored that irritating little voice inside her head that suspiciously sounded like her aunt, that not only called her a liar, but a bald-faced one at that.

As the days grew closer to Aunt Lilly's surgery, she was relieved that Jake was going to drive her and her aunt to Sheridan that weekend for her surgery. She was worried enough about her aunt, and his offer had been one that she'd gladly accepted.

Forcing Holt from her mind, Yasmine sank into work. Between running the kitchen as well as meeting with Nate and Althea, as she'd agreed to cater their wedding, life was hectic. By the time her days ended, Yasmine sank into the mattress, her muscles achy and tired.

Yet for all the hard work and the aches, and the long days, she couldn't remember a time when she'd felt more content, more fulfilled, despite the many things on her agenda she had to consider regarding her future. Along with running the kitchen and preparing a menu for the wedding—thankfully getting help from one of the local girls in town Lilly had managed to snag—she'd also reacquainted herself with the ranch.

Over the past few days, after finishing work, she left the cleanup to Jackie, the new girl Nate had found to help, trying one last time to redeem himself in Lilly's eyes for all the others who hadn't worked out.

The ranch had grown so much since her last visit,

she thought as she came home after a short ride on one of the horses she'd been given to use.

The men had recently begun to breed high-quality Braunvieh bulls with some of their prize heifers, and the income this generated had allowed them to expand the ranch.

Besides the nightly calls from Clayton, many of which she had missed, she'd kept her mind busy, tooling over the idea of a catering business, which had begun to look more and more appealing as she took her nightly rides.

After her aunt recovered, she would be bucking at the bit to return to her kitchen, and with the help of Jackie, she knew Aunt Lilly would be able to manage.

She knew soon she'd have to make a decision about her career, which road she would take.

She knew the decision wouldn't be an easy one.

Holt waited until he was riding parallel with the steer before making his move. Timing it just right, he leaped from his horse and caught the steer in a smooth head catch, taking it to the ground.

Maintaining his hold on the steer's horns, he grabbed the rope from around his waist with his gloved hand, sweat pouring down his face as he wrestled the out-of-control steer to the ground.

Not giving the animal a chance to escape, he jumped on top of its fallen body, swiftly wrapping the rope around the front two legs, securing them together, before moving to its hind legs and wrapping them securely together, establishing and maintaining control throughout the process.

Once he was sure the animal was trussed properly, unable to move, he jumped up, removed his Stetson from his head and wiped his brow with the bandanna from his back pocket.

"Damn it!" He bit out the expletive, placing his hands alongside his waist, blowing out an exhausted breath of air.

"Hell, man…I didn't know who was going to win that round… Gotta hand it to you, Holt, you would have done Dad proud!"

Holt turned toward his brother Shilah, part of his irritation evaporating at the unexpected compliment.

He'd been called in by one of the hands to help with a steer that was out of control that morning, just as he'd been about to hunt down Yasmine. Enough was enough. He was tired of the way they circled each other, both knowing they wanted each other but equally hell-bent on ignoring the attraction.

He was going to tie her down to a chair if he had to, and make her listen as he tried to explain what had happened the Saturday of her welcome-home party, as well as the night she'd seen him come home early in the morning.

He could tell from her cold look as well as the way she'd called him the hated nickname, she thought he'd come in from a night spent with a woman. Too tired to run after her and explain that he'd simply been helping Doc Crandall, the ranch's vet, bring in two calves both within hours of each other and both hard births, he'd let her think what she wanted.

That had to be the reason for her avoiding him as well as her hot-to-cold treatment in the kitchen.

He'd also been damn pissed off. He knew his reputation. Hell, he'd earned the nickname a hundred times over. But that was the past, and although he hadn't been that guy in a long time, the nickname, as well as the rep that went with it, was one he still dealt with.

Until Yasmine had reentered his life, he hadn't given a damn what others thought of him. In fact, he'd relished the nickname, as it kept most of the women with long-term dreams of happily-ever-after far away.

Again…until Yasmine.

Damn. When had that happened? he wondered, the realization that he had feelings for her, hitting him, hard, fast. When had her opinion of him begun to matter?

He had always lived his life the way he wanted, no commitments to anyone or anything unless he was the one who wanted it and he was the one calling the shots. The only time *he* was willing to bend to another's will had been to his foster father, Jed Wilde.

Jed had been the only man to prove he was worthy of that type of devotion. And then came his brothers. He loved them both, Shilah and Nate, as though they shared the same blood.

Nothing and no one came before his brothers, and no one mattered to him in the world like his brothers did, outside of Lilly. And no one ever would.

Yasmine's pretty face instantly came to mind.

He'd been trying for the better part of a week to get her alone, to explain.

And what did he do the minute he did? Mauled her like an adolescent trying to get his first piece, he thought in disgust. He had to do something. He didn't know how long his libido could take the nightly visits he received from her, via his dreams, before he went caveman and hauled her stubborn, obstinate…sexy body off to his bed.

"Yeah…that's the way to get her to think you're not the 'Penthouse,'" he muttered.

Deciding to explain things once and for all, wanting to start all over with her, he'd been seconds from hunting her down when he received a call from Jake. He was needed to help with one of the new steers they'd recently bought at auction.

Although Nate was the one they normally called in for situations like this, having done a stint in rodeo, he and Althea were going to visit the pastor for marital counseling. Any other time, that alone would have been fodder for Holt to seek his brother out just for shits and giggles and to give the once-confirmed bachelor a hard time. But now his only objective was to find Yasmine and try and fix what he had no idea how to fix.

And why he was so desperate to do so.

He ran a hand through his sweaty hair and frowned when he saw his brother staring at him as if he had two heads.

"What the hell are you staring at, Shilah?" he asked, irritably.

"Guess I forgot what it looked like."

Holt frowned. "Okay, I'll bite… What looks like?"

"When a Wilde falls in love."

"Man, go to—"

"Hey, guys, have you seen Nate?"

Before Holt could finish his sentence, both men turned when Althea came near them.

"Hey, Thea, what are you still doing hanging around? Don't you and Nate have to be in town this morning?"

"We do. Which is why I'm hunting down your brother," she replied. "Thought I'd find him here. I heard Jake asking for help with the new steer," she finished with a frown, casting a look down at the animal who now, much more docile, was being led away by one of the hands.

"Already taken care of," Shilah said, nodding toward Holt.

Althea turned her dark brown eyes in Holt's direction. "I was just in the kitchen helping Lilly and Yasmine," she said directly. "I haven't been able to talk with her as much as I would like to, with the wedding plans taking a lot of my time. Between that and her busy schedule, we've barely been able to chat."

She stopped and frowned. "And even then, I rarely see her. Seems one minute she's busy in the kitchen, and then she's gone."

Although the statement was said innocently enough, Holt caught the question behind it, but ignored Althea's not-so-subtle probes.

"Yeah, it has been long days for her. Besides, she's

always been shy. I think it may take her a while to get used to the ranch again. It can be a little overwhelming," Holt replied, evading the questions in Althea's eyes.

"Shy? Yasmine?" All three turned when Jake cut in, having come in on the tail end of the conversation after directing the men on where to move the herd.

"The Yasmine I saw at the party was anything but shy." He shook his head, laughing. "And the Yasmine out riding at night hardly seems to be overwhelmed. In fact, just the opposite. No, our caterpillar has definitely come out of her cocoon. She's a beautiful butterfly now."

Holt was two seconds from knocking the grin off Jake's face. "Beautiful butterfly? Where do you come up with shit like that, Jake? From the back of a cereal box?"

Before Jake could respond, he continued, "And what do you know about her rides?"

"I've seen her a few times. I even rode out with her a few nights ago," Jake replied. "Is that a problem?"

Althea's eyes darted back and forth between the two men, before glancing at Shilah, silently asking for help. When he only shrugged his wide shoulders, an enigmatic look on his handsome face as he closely watched his brother, Althea turned back to Jake and Holt.

"You're damn right it's a problem if—"

When he felt Althea touch his arm, his muscles bunching beneath her small hand, he glanced down at her. Had she not stepped in, he'd been seconds away from going after Jake. A worried frown marred her forehead and he forced himself to calm down.

He gave her a reassuring smile, or at least what he thought was reassuring, and stepped back.

It was then that he noticed both Jake and Shilah looking away and followed the direction of their gaze.

Yards away he saw Yasmine stomping across the field. He frowned, squinting against the sun's noontime glare.

Holt relaxed, leaning back against the railing, watching as Yasmine approached. Without his knowing it, a grin of anticipation stretched his mouth wide.

He didn't know what to expect from her, particularly after their explosive encounter in the kitchen.

She was a mass of contradictions. One minute she ran hot for him, the next minute cold as the ice that had doused her back in the kitchen.

He waited until she had entered the pasture, and without taking his eyes from her approaching figure said goodbye to Althea and the others and instructed one of the men to take over for him.

This might take a while.

When she reached him, the look on her face told him he was right. "If Jake can't take us, I can take my aunt to Sheridan myself."

He crossed his arms over his chest. "Never said you did. Or that you couldn't. It's a four-hour drive and I thought you'd like to use the time to spend with Lilly. I would think she would be anxious about the surgery. I thought you'd like to spend the time during the ride up to get her mind off of it," he said.

"And besides, who are you to tell someone they can't

take me? You're not the boss of me," she sputtered, ignoring his interjection, and he held back a grin when he saw her clamp her mouth shut, her light brown face suffusing with color at her very adolescent response.

He pushed away from the fence and walked toward her, ignoring the others, who simply stared at them both, watching their interaction.

He saw her hesitate, take a step backward before she stopped and held up her chin, one hand planted on the curve of her hip in challenge.

Good. He was just in that type of mood, he thought, relishing their encounter.

He grasped her beneath the elbow. "Let's take this somewhere else," he said, his tone brooking no argument.

Yasmine didn't know what to say, completely undone by his calm demeanor and the casual, possessive way he drew her away from the others.

So much so that she found herself meekly allowing him to drag her away from their prying eyes.

Once they'd reached a secluded area, she dug her heels in, forcing him to stop.

"Look, Jake can take me and my aunt, and if you have a problem with that, you can—" The rest of her diatribe was swallowed in his kiss.

She sputtered, pushing ineffectively at his chest. But the magic of his kiss soon turned her squirms of protest into cries of delight.

Wrapping her arms around his neck, she tunneled her

fingers through his hair and pulled him down, kissing him with all the pent-up frustration and confusion she'd felt for the past two weeks, all the longing and desire that had been building so high she felt she'd explode if she didn't feel his lips on hers.

On and on the kiss went, both of them devouring each other, until the voice of reason broke through and Yasmine pushed him away from her.

She stared up at him warily, wiping the back of her mouth with her hand.

"Stay away from me, Holt Wilde. I don't want you taking me to Sheridan, and I don't want you anywhere near me. Just go away."

He stared at her, insolently, his glance raking over her, making her feel naked and exposed. "That's not what your mouth and hands were just telling me," he said, laughing. "When you figure out what it is you want, you can give me a call. I won't come chasing after you again."

Holt didn't know what had come over him, and felt like a damn fool when he watched her sashay away, hips swinging as she whirled and walked…no, strode, away, head held high in the air.

The woman had him running hot and cold in equal measure.

Hot for her body, cold in anger when she blatantly flirted with the men as though he wasn't even there.

Although she'd pissed him off to no end, he couldn't help but appreciate the sexy sway of her hips, the way her round little bottom filled out the skirt she wore.

Despite the chilly day she'd worn a skirt and high heels. His glance fell down to the heels she wore, the way they shaped and formed her calves as she walked away. The heels not only gave her added inches, but also added a certain…sexiness to her walk.

Didn't the woman have any good sense? he wondered, his gaze continuing its traveling, past her hips, down her legs to her sexy shoes, the high heels of which were sinking in the mud as she angrily strode away.

He glanced around and saw that he wasn't the only one who appreciated the spectacular visual.

When he caught the eyes of several of his men, they hastily looked away and went back to work, noting the scowl across his face.

He turned toward Yasmine just as she was about to walk inside the house.

Jake had approached her and she stopped, looking up at him. Whatever he said made her tinkling giggle float across the field and the irrational anger knot in his gut.

Chapter 11

"They say you can take the girl from the ranch, but you can't take the ranch from the girl."

Thinking she was alone, startled, Yasmine twisted her upper torso in the saddle, glancing over her shoulder. She smiled when she saw Jake leaning against the corral.

"Oh, hey, Jake. I didn't see you there," she said, reining the horse around so that she could face him. "I was just about to put her up for the night."

As she cantered the horse closer to the fence, he hopped over it and strolled over to meet her. Standing beside the horse, he ran a hand over its mane and smiled up at Yasmine. "Still hard to believe this is the same horse Nate bought a few months ago," he said, shaking his head.

"Yeah, Holt told me she was all but wild when he bought her. He mentioned that Althea had a lot to do with her transformation," she said, and allowed him to help her dismount.

"Yeah, she had a lot to do with it. She's a hell of a woman."

As she pulled her hand away from his grasp once she was on her feet, he held on a fraction longer than necessary.

She looked up at him, a slight frown on her face, and his smile widened.

"She's not the only one," he replied.

For a brief moment, Yasmine was caught off guard by the casual compliment.

"The women on Wilde Ranch, you and Lilly, and now Althea, are all a breed apart," he finished, and she blushed slightly at the compliment.

"Why, thank you, kind sir. We try our best," she replied lightly, tipping the brim of an imaginary hat in his direction.

He laughed, tapping the end of her nose. "That's what I've always liked about you, Yas."

"What's that?" she asked, glancing up at him.

"Your sense of humor. Among other things," he said, taking the horse's reins, guiding her in the direction of the stable.

Again, Yasmine was caught off guard, causing her to stumble.

Jake caught her beneath the elbow, righting her.

With a mumbled thank-you she smiled slightly, when

she saw him staring down at her with an odd look on his face.

"I must look a mess," she said, self-consciously running a hand over her disheveled hair.

She'd been hard at work the entire day.

Truth be told, much of that hard work had been in avoiding Holt, yesterday as well as today. She'd told herself it wasn't because she was afraid to be alone with him, it was just that she didn't have anything to say to him.

Yeah, right, her inner voice mocked her.

"No. In fact, you look beautiful," Jake said, the smile on his face broadening, the appreciation in his eyes as his glance slid over her unmistakable.

At his response, Yasmine paused and looked up at him.

"Thank you, Jake," she said, suddenly on unsure ground.

"Mind if I walk with you to put her away?"

She forced a smile and nodded her head.

As they walked toward the stable, they chatted lightly, Jake asking how things were going and that he'd heard about her catering the wedding.

"Yeah, that came out of the blue." She laughed, walking alongside him. "When she asked, well…I couldn't say no. Nate is like family," she said softly. "Everyone here is like family."

"Including me?" he asked.

"Of course."

"It's been a long time since you've been home, Yasmine. It's good to know you think of me the same as you do the others."

Yasmine felt the uneasiness grow but pushed it away. This was Jake. They'd grown up together and he was as close as a brother to her as the Wildes were. Well, as much as Nate and Shilah were, she thought.

"So much has changed around the ranch," she said, changing the subject. When they passed a large oak tree, a rope around an old tire suspended from one of the thick, overhead branches, she said, "Seems like just yesterday we were all swinging from that old tire," and they both laughed in memory.

"Yeah, I was trying to get your attention back then, but that didn't work any more than it has since you came back."

Although she wasn't entirely surprised by his admission, she hadn't known he'd liked her when they were younger.

He smiled down at her once they reached the stall. "Yeah," he admitted sheepishly, running a hand through his hair. "But even then, you only had eyes for Holt. Guess nothing's changed, huh, Yas?"

From the moment she'd returned home, she'd caught the way Jake looked at her whenever he was near. At first when the thought had come to her mind that he was attracted to her, she'd brushed it away, thinking she was seeing things that weren't there, that it was simply her imagination, but now she wondered if it were more.

She didn't know what to say. And neither did she

know that anyone, outside of her aunt, knew of her girlhood crush on Holt.

"I—uh…"

He shook his head, the smile dying on his lips. "You don't have to say anything, Yasmine. I knew your heart belonged to him. And now…well, like I said, guess nothing's changed."

When he was set to guide the horse inside, she placed a hand over his, stalling him.

"I never knew. Had I known, well…" She allowed the sentence to dangle, glancing over his face.

Unlike Holt, Jake wasn't handsome in the traditional sense of the word. His strong aquiline nose, broken sometime in his youth, dominated an angular face. His dark, inky-black hair was cut close to his head. When dampened with sweat, as it was now, the ends curled up, forming curls that covered his head. His mouth was a slashing line, usually somber in looks, unless he smiled. But his eyes… Jake's eyes were a magnet.

Light green, the lashes surrounding them were inky-black, matching the color of his hair.

Like the brothers, Jake was tall, well over six feet in height, with powerful shoulders that tapered to a lean waist.

As she said to him, had she known, and if she hadn't fallen for Holt all those years ago…

He placed a finger beneath her chin and raised it so her glance met his. She saw him lower his face and turned her face away enough so that he only kissed her softly on the corner of her mouth.

"Well, there it is," he said, and in his voice she heard a certain sadness. "Doesn't mean we can't be friends, does it? And maybe we can give that old tire another ride. Sound like fun?" he asked, and she grinned, her mood lightening along with his attempt to put her at ease.

"Tonight seems as good a time as any. Give me a minute to put the horse away," she replied, grinning up at him.

"Why don't I give you a hand with that? We can get to that swing that much faster."

"You're on!"

Just then a sound alerted them that they weren't alone, and seconds later Holt emerged from around the stable, walking toward them, his stride unhurried.

"Kinda late to be out riding horses, don't you think, Yas?"

Although he asked her the question, his voice mild, his gaze was directly on Jake. But as he came out of the shadows and withdrew his Stetson, there was nothing mild about the look on his face. His bright blue eyes were blazing with fury beneath the halogen light.

Yasmine took a step back, coming up short when she felt Jake's hand on her elbow, steadying her.

Holt's gaze followed the action. A muscle ticked in the corner of his sensual mouth.

"Let her go," he said, his voice pitched low.

The sound of his voice and his quiet anger startled Yasmine so much she gasped.

"Holt, man, wha—"

"I said let her go, Jake." His voice was cold, unyielding. "Yasmine and I have some unfinished business to discuss."

The air around them grew suddenly colder, and Yasmine wrapped her arms around her body in reaction.

Jake moved her to the side and faced Holt.

"I don't know what your problem is, but we can discuss this civilly or…"

"Or?"

Holt advanced on them and Yasmine snapped out of her momentary daze. She knew, instinctually, that she needed to put as much distance between herself and Jake as she could. Quickly. Walking forward, she placed an arm on Holt's forearm, feeling the muscles bunch beneath her fingertips.

She turned to Jake, forcing her mouth to stretch into what she hoped was a semblance of a smile. "I'm sorry, Jake. Holt's right. I completely forgot about our…uh, plans. Maybe we can swing from the branch another time?" she asked, infusing levity into her voice.

Jake stood still, looking from Yasmine to Holt and back again, before nodding his head, his features set. He placed his Stetson back on his head and focused his gaze on Yasmine, a curious look on his face.

"Okay, I'm going to hold you to that," he said softly, with a corner of his mouth lifting. "I'll take care of your horse," he said with a curt nod in Holt's direction. He took the reins and guided the horse away.

The minute he rounded the corner and they were

alone, Yasmine spun around, placing her hands on her hips, and faced off with Holt.

"What in the hell was *that* all about?"

He took two steps forward until his big body brushed against hers, crowding her so that she was forced to take a step back.

"I don't know who you think you are, ordering me around like that," she boldly went on, pushing down the apprehension at the look on his face, his entire demeanor, and continued, one foot tapping against the ground. "I don't know what's wrong with you. You think you can ignore me for days at a time and then go all caveman. And if you think a simple kiss gives you the right to—"

Holt grabbed Yasmine by the waist, the air escaping from her mouth in a whoosh when he hauled her close and slanted his mouth over hers, effectively ending her angry tirade.

Chapter 12

Yasmine struggled, planting her balled fist against his chest and shoving as hard as she could.

He didn't move an inch. It was as though she were trying to move a two-ton block of cement, as effective as she was.

He grabbed her hands at the wrists and shackled them with one of his large hands, raising them together high above her head, and continued his sensual assault on her mouth.

Her body slumped and her mouth softened, yielding to him.

She heard a very masculine grunt of approval, felt his hold on her loosen, felt his lips soften, and with a groan, he slipped his tongue between the seam of her lips, asking for entry.

She arched her back away from the barn door, into his embrace…and with as much force as she could, kneed him, and quickly jumped out of his hold while he was distracted.

"Damn it, Yasmine!" He bit out a much more explicit oath and jumped away, grabbing his thigh.

Although she'd missed her target by a few inches, a grin of satisfaction stretched her mouth wide.

She didn't have time to savor the moment.

When she saw the gleam in his bright blue eyes, she knew retribution was right around the corner. With a yelp, she evaded his outstretched hands and pushed aside the barn door, slamming it shut behind her before he could reach her, and ran inside looking for cover.

Her heartbeat was racing, blood pumping strongly through her veins after she spun and immediately began to run, looking for a place to duck and cover.

She heard his curse behind her.

She didn't have long; soon he would be after her. She found a small space near the back of the barn and dived into the hay, hoping he wouldn't come looking in the place she'd found.

Yasmine stayed in that position for as long as possible. When she heard no more sounds, no footsteps, nothing but the sounds of the few horses in the stable, she released her breath, expecting to feel relief that he had left.

Instead of relief, she felt a stinging disappointment, the adrenaline slowly leaving her body.

Slowly she rose to her feet, and walked out into

the main aisle, looking around just to make sure he was gone.

She'd taken no more than two steps when two large, strong hands grabbed her by the waist, and taking her with him, the two went down onto the ground, their fall cushioned by the soft hay.

"Can't get away from me that easily, Yas…I've tackled bigger prey than you when I played ball," he said, grunting when she tried to connect again with that part she'd missed earlier.

"Fool me once. Not again." He laughed roughly, flipping her body around so that she was beneath him, trapped.

"A simple kiss, Yas?" he asked, his voice low.

He leaned down, brushing his face against the side of her cheek in a back-and-forth motion, the stubble from his cheek a rough caress against her skin.

Yasmine closed her eyes and inhaled deeply, determined not to allow his nearness…his scent, his overwhelming masculinity, to make her succumb.

She swallowed back the moan of satisfaction when he bit down on her earlobe lightly, before his tongue snaked out and licked a hot path down the side of her neck.

"Wha—what do you want from me?" To her own ears the question was more like a plea than anything else.

His tongue continued its deadly assault, trailing a path from her earlobe to the corner of her mouth. "Whatever you want to give me," he whispered.

"Holt…" His name was drawn out on a long sigh before he recaptured her mouth.

"God, Yasmine…I've been wanting to touch you, to feel you like this, for so long," he said, thumbing a rough caress across one of her nipples. With a growl he bent down, moved the flimsy lace of her bra aside and drew her nipple and most of the surrounding aureole deep inside his mouth.

Yasmine cried out, her body arching sharply away from the hay, pressing herself closer to his questing mouth.

"Holt…" She breathed his name, her body on fire from his nibbling kisses and caresses.

She placed a hand out, between them, against his chest. She turned her face away.

She couldn't get caught up in him. Not again. His odd hot-and-cold treatment was too much for her, she needed to put him…them, her feelings for him, in the past. Where they belonged.

"We can't—" Again her words were cut off when he placed his mouth over hers, pressing his hot tongue inside. He turned her face back around, forcing her to look at him.

"I know. This is crazy. The way I'm feeling, the way you're making me go wild, just from looking at you." In his voice she heard the confusion she herself felt, as though he didn't understand what was going on between them any more than she did.

"And when I saw you with Jake…the way he's been

sniffing around you for the last few days…I lost it." The admission seemed to be torn from him.

He guided his other hand down her waist, lightly toying with her belly button before pressing his large palm at the top of her mound, pushing against her.

"Hmm…Holt, what…" she stopped, panting "…what are you doing?" she cried, and held her breath when she felt his hand ease the zipper down, pushing the waistband of her jeans to the side.

"Making you feel good, I hope," he mumbled against the underside of her breast. When his finger delved inside, past the thin cotton of her panties, and found its mark, she inhaled a long, harsh breath.

His breathing, hot against her skin, grew more labored as he worked his finger deeper inside her clenching warmth. When he found her clitoris and lightly pinched it between two fingers, she felt the ease of her arousal flow, past his fingers and down the inside of her legs.

He released her breasts, the nipple plopping out of his mouth in a loud pop as he trailed his tongue up her body. He reached the hollow of her throat and licked her, swirling his tongue inside the tiny indenture before continuing the path up her neck, suckling her chin until she whimpered. He released her chin and continued his sensual laving, ending at the corner of her mouth.

"Do you like what I'm doing to you, Yas?" He breathed the words against the corner of her mouth. Not giving her a chance to respond, he placed his thumbs inside the waistband of her jeans, and in one yank pulled them down, lifting her enough so that he could take them up and over her bottom.

Immediately his hands went back to work. Pulling aside her panties, he inserted one long finger deep inside her body, slowly rotating it, until it was all Yasmine could do to hold back a scream. In and out he plunged his finger, one, then adding a second, pressing in and out of her welcoming heat.

Yasmine whimpered, squirming around his thick fingers, her head tossing back and forth against the rough hay as she bit down hard on her bottom lip, afraid that if she didn't she'd wake everyone on the ranch with her cries.

He released her mouth, uttering a rough laugh against her cheek. "Go ahead, baby, let it out. No one can hear us out here… Let go, Yas," he said.

He hooked his hands beneath her knees, lifting them and her wider, and snaked his body down until she felt his warm, heavy breath fan the hair covering her mound.

She swallowed hard. "Holt…no, no, baby, I—" She moaned, the sound little more than a whimper when she felt his tongue snake between the seam of her lips, long…slick…and hot.

As he licked and sucked, worshipping her in the most intimate way, Yasmine's breath grew ragged, her head spinning out of control. He was merciless in his sensual attack, alternating between playful short swipes of his tongue and long, languid strokes until she felt the fire within burn, blaze out of control.

She grabbed his head, not to push him away but to force him even closer. She heard his ragged masculine laughter as he gave her what she wanted, God, what she'd needed for so long, wringing from her everything she had.

Her walls tightened, her womb contracting as she felt the beginnings of her release.

As she came, her body starting to shake out of control, from a distance she heard the sound of paper ripping, and moments later, as the orgasm slammed into her, felt the broad head of his shaft at her entry.

Her eyes slammed open as his cock began to push past her vaginal lips and slowly he fed her inches of the broad tip.

"Oh God, oh God, oh God," she chanted as she accepted him. He was so thick, so hard, it soon became uncomfortable, and a panic set in and she fought against him, panting out, "No, Holt…you're too big, I can't—"

His mouth slammed over hers, pushing past her lips, his tongue swept inside her mouth, overcoming her objections as he slowly pushed more of himself deep inside her body. She felt her body rebel, tighten up, her inner muscles clamping down on his shaft, forcing him to stop his invasion.

He pulled his mouth away from hers, and she felt his hands on either side of her face, his thumbs caressing.

"Open for me, Yasmine. Please," he said. Yasmine heard the ragged plea as though from a distance and opened her eyes. "I'll never hurt you. I promise you, baby. Please…"

Their breaths were both coming out in gasps, and Yasmine ran panicked eyes over his face, so close to hers.

She could barely see his eyes in the shadows, yet the sincerity in the deep blue depths reached out to her.

"Relax, baby…just relax." He panted the words, the fine ends of his nostrils flaring as he tried to calm her. As her eyes trained on the small tic in the corner of his mouth, she felt the trembling coming from his big body so close to hers.

Still on fire from his invasion, she struggled to accept him, her body taut, arched like a bow and quivering.

"You trust me, don't you, Yas?" he asked. Yasmine glanced up at him, her eyes scanning over him, seeing the hair that had fallen forward to lie on his damp forehead.

She slowly nodded her head, and saw the relief in his eyes.

"Good, baby. I'll go slow…I'll make it good for you. I promise," he said. With that he leaned down and captured one of her breasts, tugging her nipple into his mouth and suckling. His other hand reached between their wet bodies, found the nub of her core and slowly rotated the bud until Yasmine whimpered, her body arching into his caresses.

Slowly he continued to feed her more of his shaft in slow, sweet increments until he had filled her, so deep she felt him tap the back of her womb. Once he'd hit the back of her, he paused, lifting his body away from her, his arms bracketing her on both sides.

"Do you want me, Yas?" he asked, sweat falling from his chest to splatter like rain on dry ground to land on her breasts. She swallowed and nodded. She saw him close his eyes briefly before opening them. The look blazing in their depths made her heart contract and her legs clench, bringing him even deeper inside her body.

He laughed roughly, planting a kiss on the corner of her mouth before moving away. "If you keep doing that, this won't last long, baby." The clarity of his statement was easy to figure out. She felt a blush stain her cheeks even as her body, as though with a will of its own, sought his, grinding against his hips, her hips slowly rotating against his.

When he groaned again, this time deeper in his throat, the sound akin to an animal, a part of Yasmine, that part deep inside that was universal to all women, surged in triumph; that she had reduced a man like Holt to this state was a heady feeling.

"So tight. God, you feel so good on me, Yas," he rasped.

His mouth came down on hers as he slid in that one last inch, driving home.

Yasmine's body arched sharply away from the soft hay, her muffled cries absorbed by his mouth as his thrusts became more forceful.

As her breasts pressed into his chest he tore his mouth from hers and latched on to one, tugging her nipple inside his mouth, pressing it against the roof of his mouth, sending the cream to ease down her leg, easing his entry into her portal.

"Holt!" she screamed, no longer caring who could hear her as the pleasure began to spiral deep within her body.

He placed his hands back beneath her knees, lifting her body away from the ground, and drove into her, his hips like pistons, driving deeper and deeper inside her, subtly arranging her body along his for their mutual pleasure.

She felt it the minute the orgasm began. As he continued to pound into her, the power of his thrusts sending her body into overdrive, she reached up and grasped him around the neck, pulling him down on top of her, so their bodies moved of one accord. He smoothly caught her rhythm, twisting their bodies until they lay on their sides, facing one another.

Hiking one of her legs up, he placed it over his hip, digging into her at a new angle, his thrusts now tight, controlled, her legs forced closer together, her clitoris in direct contact with the end of his shaft as the tip was tapping against her spot.

It was too much.

Her body went nuclear.

"Yes…yes…yesssss," she screamed, frantically grabbing at him as the orgasm began to unfurl. His hands gripped the undersides of her ass, digging into the flesh as he continued his sensual assault, grinding into her, his powerful thrusts overwhelming her.

When the orgasm hit, she screamed, grinding against

him, trying to get as close as possible to his body. As though from a distance she heard his roar, as he, too, gave in to the climax. His grip on her hips became nearly painful as he issued one, two, three more thrusts before he went over the edge into mindless bliss.

Chapter 13

Holt had suspected from the moment he'd kissed Yasmine that sex between them would be amazing.

But never in his wildest imagination did he think he would have had the type of mind-blowing sex he'd had with her.

He ran a hand through his hair.

After their first coupling, they'd allowed their breathing to calm, their hearts to return to normal. But the minute he'd felt her soft, round bottom nudge against his shaft as she lay in front of him, his cock had hardened, stiffening on cue.

He'd reached for his jeans, withdrawing the foil package, and ripped it open with his teeth. After donning the protection, he'd placed a kiss on the side of her neck. She'd stirred and moaned softly when he'd captured a nipple in his mouth and suckled on the hardening nub. He'd eased his body down until his face was level with her mound. Taking a cursory swipe against her slickening lips, her essence trickled over his mouth.

He couldn't get enough of her. Her smell, her taste… everything about her was like a drug to him. A habit he had no intention of kicking anytime soon.

When he felt her soft hands reach down and cover the back of his head, urging him closer to her nectar, he'd lost it. After one more taste of her honey, he'd drawn away, moving back up her body until he lay between her opened thighs.

He captured her mouth, transferring her own flavor to her, licking and biting at the lushness of her mouth.

"How about you take over the ride this time?" he asked, whispering the words low, against the corner of her mouth.

"Wha—what do you mean?" Her voice was husky and low; it brushed over his senses, making his shaft even harder. He gritted his teeth.

Smoothly Holt repositioned them so that she straddled him. Taking her hands within his, he levered her up so that she sat astride him. Slowly he pressed the tip of his shaft inside her quivering opening, going far enough in that her eyes widened, her mouth forming a perfect O.

"Ohhh." She sighed the word on a long breath.

"Are you okay?" he asked, worried, remembering how difficult it had been the first time for her to accept all of him. "It's good?"

He saw her throat work as she swallowed. Her eyes

fluttered closed, her mouth and small breaths escaped her partially opened mouth. She swiped her tongue out, wetting her lush lower rim, and nodded her head. "Yes... yes, it's good," she whispered.

That was all he needed to hear. Although careful, he made short work of feeding her the rest of his shaft, going deep until he felt the tip of his cock brush against her womb. He bit back a groan when she squirmed on top of him, adjusting herself for a better fit.

"Baby..." He bit out the warning and her eyes flashed open. She glanced over his face, taking in his pinched features and a smile, very small, lifted the corners of her mouth.

"Is it good for you?" she asked, and although her voice was hesitant, unsure, there was a wicked gleam in her eyes as he answered her in action, lifting her bottom slowly...so painfully slow, up and away from his shaft, and just as slowly eased her back down until she was seated fully on him.

"Minx," he growled, and grasped her by the hips to better anchor her on him.

Biting her bottom lip, she looked down at him and slowly began to undulate, her hips moving in perfect harmony with his. When he raised his hips, lifting them both from the floor, she arched back, catching his rhythm easily. The wet, tight feel of her warmth surrounding him had him groaning loudly, like a boy getting his first piece. She moved so well, undulating her hips, clenching her thighs, forcing his shaft into tighter alignment with her body.

His hands on her hips gripped her tightly as she caught his thrusts and gave them back to him. He watched as she grew bolder, the way she watched him as they moved as one. He reached up, pinched one of her nipples, watching in fascination as it grew longer. He slipped a hand between their tightly joined bodies and found her clit, and as he massaged the hard nub of her nipple, he rolled and lightly pinched her clit until she moaned harshly in the quiet barn.

It was incredible, the way she moved, the way she made him feel.

She continued to undulate her hips, moving her back, her hips, working his body like a pro. He continued to plow inside her sweetness, feeling his balls tingle, the sensation telling him he was close to orgasm.

Not yet.

With a feral growl, he raised his body, grasped her by the back of her head and slammed his mouth over hers, twisting their bodies until she lay beneath him. She laughed lightly, and he pulled her bottom lip into his mouth, biting the lushness, not enough to hurt but enough that she felt the sting.

"Oooh!" she whimpered, and it was his turn to utter a low, masculine laugh.

"I'll take over now," he said, and pulled her lip into his mouth, laving the inner rim, soothing the small hurt.

"Oh, yeah?" she asked huskily.

"Yeah."

"Mmm…" she murmured on a long sigh of pleasure

when he lifted her legs and placed them around his waist.

Grinding inside her welcoming warmth, he alternated his thrusts between short and shallow, and long and deep.

"Yasmine. So hot. So sweet," he growled again when she met his deep thrust. "So tight."

Her breathing became shallow, her cries of passion louder as he continued to thrust.

Holt chose that moment to press his hand against her pelvic bone, as his fingers continued toying with her clitoris, and he felt the moment she broke.

Her body became stiff, her nails scoring into his back so deeply he knew he'd bear the marks from her passion in the morning. When she screamed her release, he lifted her bottom completely off the ground and stroked deep and hard inside her. Her head fell back, her neck straining as she accepted his thrusts, his fingers at work on her clit, unrelenting, until he'd wrung out every sensation from her. Until she lay back weak and boneless on the floor.

One more thrust and he went over the edge along with her, roaring out his release.

Completely satiated, he slumped down on her, spent. It was long moments before he could muster enough strength to move away, placing her in front of his body, her soft bottom nestled against his groin.

He grabbed a blanket and covered them, and minutes later allowed sleep to claim him.

As she lay in front of him now, the soft globes of

her buttocks cushioned against his groin, he absently feathered his hand down her arm, lost in thought.

Watching her in the kitchen earlier that day, the way she gave herself wholeheartedly to her passion of cooking, had also given him an inkling that when she gave her all, it was nothing short of spectacular.

When he'd first kissed her, her soft lips and shy smile had told him she was a woman who, if she were in the hands of the right man, would be a dangerous woman indeed.

When she'd yelled at him in the middle of the corral, in front of his men, her eyes blazing, her hands on her hips as she told him exactly what she thought of him, he knew she was a woman with hidden fire.

But never would he have imagined that making love to her could be like this.

He closed his eyes, clenching his jaw, remembering the way she felt on him. How tight she was.

So tight, it was as though she'd never…

Damn. The way her eyes had widened, the fearful look in her eye, the panicky way she'd beat against his chest, demanding him to get off of her…

She was a virgin.

Scratch that. She *had* been a virgin.

He bit out an expletive.

When she sighed softly, he glanced down at her.

No sooner had they orgasmed than she slumped down, her head falling down on his chest. Feeling uncertain how she felt after their lovemaking—a first for him— he'd said her name, only to hear her soft sighs.

She'd fallen asleep.

He'd spent the next minutes watching her as they slept. Running a hand through his hair, he'd repositioned her so that she lay again in front of him and covered their bodies with the blanket he'd found before, unsure what to do next.

Although the stables were heated, he didn't want to stay any longer, the thought of someone accidentally coming across them one he knew would embarrass Yasmine.

As far as he was concerned, he didn't care who came across them. He had no regrets about what they did last night.

He moved, wincing slightly.

What they'd done all night long, he thought, remembering in hot detail their lovemaking throughout the night.

He glanced back down at her.

During their lovemaking, her hair had come out of the neat ponytail she'd placed it in, and now lay in wild curls around her face. Her lashes, so long they seemed unreal, fanned against her cheeks, one hand tucked beneath her cheek as she laid her head on his chest.

He debated allowing her to rest longer. She looked so beautiful, so at peace, lying there.

He brought her body closer to his, spooning against her as he brought the blanket over her breasts.

It wasn't supposed to happen like this.

Yes, he knew that he was going to have her. From the moment he saw her again at the airport, he knew he would have to taste her, to sample her, to see if she was as good as she looked.

He'd been caught completely unaware by the power of their lovemaking, the way his mind, body and spirit had been teleported to another place.

He laughed, humorlessly. If his brothers could hear him mentally waxing poetic, they'd laugh their asses off. Shilah was the poetic, sensitive one. Nathan was the brooding one.

And him?

Holt shook his head, running the tips of his fingers along the soft skin on her arm. He was the one who kept it all in perspective; the one who could shake off anything with a laugh; the one who always had a comeback for any situation.

The one who never let things get under his skin, who could walk away from any person, any situation, without a backward glance. Onward and upward…and on to the next one, had always been his motto, from as early as he could remember.

Except when it came to his brothers and their ranch.

His early life with his mother and an absentee father, and their constant moving from place to place, had made it easy for Holt to never put down any roots, to take life as it came. When Celia, his mother, had told him that final time she had found a gig in California and that when she got settled she'd send for him, he'd only nodded his head and turned away, settling his ragged backpack on the bed he'd been given at the group home where she'd dumped him, and hadn't bothered to turn her way when she said goodbye. When she'd awkwardly tried to hug him, he'd returned her embrace just as stiffly, just anxious for her to go.

From that moment on, he'd stopped thinking about the what-ifs and everything that came with them, and learned to deal with the moment in front of him. To make the most of what life brought his way.

He didn't need a degree in psychology to tell him he had "unresolved issues," as most of the talk-show psychologists liked to call it. Whatever the cause or reason, as he matured he'd always found it better to enjoy what life gave him for the moment and give no thought for what the next day would bring. Life was a lot easier that way.

"What's that Bible passage Miss Lilly is always quoting about taking no thought for tomorrow, let it take care of itself?" He posed the question to the dark in a low voice, unconsciously running a hand over the silky skin of Yasmine's exposed arm.

Seemed like a pretty good way to look at things, he thought.

When he heard one of the horses' soft neigh in a nearby stall, he glanced up, and through the small window at the top of the stall saw the early sunrise begin to peek through the lattice blinds.

Soon, the ranch would be up and stirring. He glanced back down at Yasmine, her head still cushioned on his chest. Bending close, he moved aside her damp bangs and placed a kiss on her forehead.

As he watched her sleep, her soft curls fanning his naked chest, he hated the thought of waking her. To wake her meant answering questions. Questions he wasn't sure he was ready to answer. He hadn't figured it all out in his own mind yet. He didn't know what her expectations were after what they'd shared. Hell, he didn't even know his own.

She had been so responsive to him. So trusting that he would take care of her.

Even in sleep, her hand was placed over his chest in an unconscious possessive gesture.

The thought brought him up short. His way of thinking, taking things as they came and never getting serious about anything outside his family and their ranch, had taken a beating after last night with Yas. He never thought making love could be like that, could take him to a place he'd dreamed about in his fantasies, a place outside the real world.

As soon as the whimsical thought hit, he drew back mentally. "Shit, man, pull up. Again, if the brothers knew what you were thinking, you'd never hear the end of it."

Last night had been something they'd both enjoyed, something that had been building since she'd come home. Something that had been as inevitable as the sun rising.

But that was it. No more, no less.

He ignored the inner mocking laughter echoing in his mind.

"Yasmine," he whispered, and kissed the corner of

her mouth, unable to resist. "Baby, we'd better get up. Sun's coming up. Time to wake up."

It was time to wake up. For both of them.

Chapter 14

Yasmine yawned and opened her eyes, immediately frowning as the bright light streamed down from the skylight.

She closed her eyes, sighing, stretching her upper torso and snuggling back down into the soft mattress. A second later her eyes flew open.

Her glance fell down to her chest, feeling the heavy weight across them. Lying crosswise over her exposed breasts was a thick, muscular forearm. She looked farther down the bed.

The top of the overstuffed down comforter barely covered their entwined bodies.

She blushed when she felt his shaft, although softened, still thick, nestled against her bottom.

Oh God…what had she done, she thought, frantically trying to orient herself to her environment.

She moved slightly, wincing when the small movement caused an ache between her legs.

Or what hadn't she done, she mentally corrected herself, glancing over her shoulder and seeing Holt's face, or at least the part that wasn't buried in the back of her neck.

She felt his breath blow warm air across her neck, and suppressed a shiver as her treacherous nipples responded as though on cue.

Her thoughts quickly went back to what had happened the night before, memories rushing down on her, causing both the blush and the ache between her legs to increase tenfold.

After they'd made love, she vaguely recalled him helping her to gather her clothes and the two of them leaving the barn.

The way he'd made love to her had been unlike anything she'd thought in her wildest fantasies, so unreal, so hot and amazing…unlike anything she could have imagined in her most erotic dreams.

She bit her lip, uncertain what to do yet, wondering if he knew he'd been the first for her.

That he was the first wasn't something she was ashamed of. It wasn't as though she'd been saving herself for him, it just hadn't happened before.

She mentally shrugged, thinking if he asked her that would be her response.

As though he would, she thought.

He probably hadn't even noticed.

The thought was sobering.

She was well aware that most of the women, if not all, knew the score with him. He was in it for a good time, he'd never made any secret of the fact.

And she was no different than any of the rest.

And now it was the morning after. So clichéd, she thought, her brows coming together in a frown, wondering how or what she'd say to him.

She wouldn't even let him think she expected anything more from him than what he'd given her last night. She wasn't embarrassed, nor did she regret what they'd done. It happened.

But why did the thought leave her feeling empty? she wondered. Gradually she allowed her eyes to close, her body sore, her mind weary from the mental gymnastics she'd just put it through.

Holt lay quietly behind Yasmine, the subtle shift in her body posture alerting him the moment she'd awakened. He waited for her to turn to him. One minute stretched into the next until he realized after he heard her soft snores that she wasn't going to.

He didn't know whether to be relieved or not.

At any rate it gave him longer to think about what he'd say to her, how they'd go forward... She'd been a virgin. Had he known she'd never been with a man before he never would have… Before he could finish the thought, he knew it was a lie.

Last night would have happened, whether he had known or not. There was no way he could have walked away from the temptation of her body.

He felt her stir, and immediately his fingers began running up and down her arm in an unconscious, soothing motion.

No, he couldn't, he wouldn't have been able to walk away from her. They'd gone too far for that.

He just would have tried to make the experience more…classy, he thought, grimacing, thinking how her first time had been in a damn barn.

He thought of the women he'd brought there, from the time he'd had his first sexual experience.

But Yasmine wasn't anything like the many other women he'd bedded. She was sexy, smart, funny… unique. She defied comparison.

He glanced down at her, felt her adjust herself against him as he lay spooned behind her. When he felt his cock stir, he ignored it. He'd been hard for her on a regular basis, so much so that he'd begun to get used to being that way whenever she was around.

Again, thinking of it being her first time, he wondered what she would expect of him, if anything. Had she been saving herself for that special man?

Holt didn't fool himself into thinking he was some knight in shining armor. Again, most of the women he was with knew the score, he was in it for a good time, and that was it.

He ran his fingers lightly over Yasmine's smooth brown arm, past her small waist and lush hips where the sheet barely covered her.

He would enjoy their time together for as long as they had.

"Hey, about what happened the other night…"

Holt reined in his horse after instructing the men, whirled around and faced Jake. His first inclination was to punch him dead in the mouth, remembering the way he'd felt when he saw him with Yasmine. Removing his Stetson, he wiped the sweat away from his forehead and jammed it back on, and waited for Jake to speak instead.

"Look, I didn't know you two had something going on, man. Had I known I never would have—" Jake stopped, removing his hat as well before running a hand through his hair, dampened with sweat.

The entire morning, Holt as well as most of the men had been running cattle from their north pasture to the south, and the day hadn't allowed him to think about much more than the hard work at hand.

But he'd caught the looks Jake had given him whenever their paths had crossed, and the tension between them was palpable. His brothers had noticed as well; he'd seen the glances they'd exchanged as the day wore on, yet neither one had said anything.

They all knew each other too well not to have noticed the tension between him and Jake. Jake was as much a part of the ranch as any of them.

Holt had known Jake from the time they were boys, as Jake's father had been the foreman on the ranch. Not long after his mother had passed away when Jake was in high school, Jake had come to live with his father in one of the guest cottages on the sprawling ranch. When his father had retired, Jake had then taken over the job as foreman. Although he had his own home in town, he continued to live primarily on the ranch in the small cottage.

To say he was as much family as Holt's own brothers was an apt statement.

"Look, it's fine. Just a misunderstanding."

"Is that all it was? Looked like more than that to me."

"And if it is—"

He held up both hands. "Just asking." He stopped, frowned and forged on. "Yasmine is special, Holt. She's not like the others."

"You don't need to tell me that."

Holt was beginning to get pissed, the underlying threat one he didn't take well. "Whatever is going on between me and Yasmine is our business. And Yasmine is a big girl, I think she can handle herself."

"I'm not saying she can't, Holt. Just thought I'd throw that out there," he said.

"I'm throwing back that I can take care of my woman."

"Is that what she is for you?"

Holt said nothing more. The realization was hitting him in two ways: one was that it was none of Jake's damn business what Yasmine was to him. The other was the realization that although he was normally the one to want to retreat, the one who didn't want to put a label on his relationships, with Yasmine he found that he wanted that, wanted to give a name to what they were to one another.

The thought was sobering.

Chapter 15

"Want a little company?"

With a mild start, Yasmine glanced away from the large bay window in her bedroom, where she'd been staring out, sightless, for the past thirty minutes, to see her aunt standing in her doorway.

She'd been so wrapped in her own thoughts she hadn't heard Lilly open the door and enter. She moved away, walking toward her aunt.

"Aunt Lilly, you shouldn't be out of bed!" Once she'd reached her, Yasmine placed her hand beneath her aunt's elbow and guided her inside.

"Girl, I'm not an invalid, quit fussing over me," Lilly admonished, yet Yasmine noticed she accepted her assistance.

She frowned deeply, worried when she felt how

much her aunt was favoring her leg, her limp strongly pronounced. Once she'd helped her aunt to sit on the bed, Yasmine sat near her and crossed her legs beneath her.

"Jackie seems to be working out okay. I think she'll be able to handle things while we're gone," Yasmine said, planting a smile on her face. "Of course she can't handle things as well as we…I mean you do," she said, laughing. "But I'm sure everything will be okay."

"Hmm…" was Lilly's only response.

"And when we get back, I'll be back in the kitchen and before you know it, in a few weeks, you'll be back on your feet and I'm sure wanting your kitchen back."

"Mmm-hmm."

"Of course, I will stay as long as you need me, before I, uh…head back to New York." Yasmine turned and faced her, quickly reassuring her aunt. "I have everything under control with work. I spoke with the producers of the show and everything is still a go, they fully understand. And of course I've spoken with Clayton, as well."

When her aunt said nothing more, Yasmine continued, outlining her course of action and her plans to return to New York.

"That or the show. I haven't quite decided which." She shrugged. "Maybe I can do both." She sighed, her shoulders slumping the smallest bit.

Just a few short weeks ago, she'd been on cloud nine with the way her career had taken off in ways she'd never imagined it would in such a short time.

"It's a dream come true. I can't wait to get back. I—"

"What's on your mind, Pooh?" Lilly asked gently, breaking into her monologue.

Immediately Yasmine stopped speaking, the nickname taking her back in time to when she was a young girl. She blinked back the sudden tears that burned the back of her eyes. "You haven't called me that in years," she replied softly.

She remembered the first time her aunt had given her the nickname. It had been soon after she'd come to stay with her. Lilly had given her a Winnie the Pooh stuffed animal and told her to hug it tight at night, whenever she thought of her parents. Yasmine remembered the number of times she'd done that, holding the bear close as she cried into it, taking it around with her everywhere she went that first year she'd grown so attached to it. In a way, it had become her lifeline, and whenever anyone saw her, Pooh was not far away. So much so, that her aunt had taken to calling her Pooh.

She glanced toward the nightstand. Head drooped down from the years of being handled and its clothes threadbare, the stuffed animal sat. On occasion she still needed the bear, remembering how she'd slept with it just last night, hugging it close, as she'd done all those years ago, as though it was some kind of lucky charm that could make all her worries, doubts and fears go away with a wave of his furry little hand.

If only it could be that easy.

"That seems like a lifetime ago," she said, glancing at her aunt, referring to the nickname as well as that time in her life when she'd needed the lifeline. Remembering how she'd slept with the bear, she realized, maybe not so long ago.

When she glanced back at her aunt she saw the fleeting look of sadness in her dark brown eyes, drawing her out of her own problems. "Aunt Lilly?" She paused. "Is everything okay?"

"You've grown so much, baby. You're not that sad little girl anymore." A small smile tilted her aunt's mouth. "I couldn't be prouder of you." There was a husky quality to her voice. She ran worried eyes over Yasmine. "I couldn't love you any more if you were my own child. Even though you don't need me as much as you once did, I'll always be here for you."

Yasmine reached over and placed her arms around her aunt. "God, no! I'll always need you, Mama Lilly. You're the only person in this world I have ever had to lean on. The only one who cares about me." She swallowed the tears clogging the back of her throat, her voice shaky. "And you were…still are, the best mother a woman could ever have. I will always need you."

For long moments the women hugged, and Yasmine allowed the tears to fall. Tears for the little girl who'd lost her parents…for the little girl hopelessly in love with a man for years, one who didn't…or couldn't, love her back the way she longed for him to. The way she craved.

With a soothing pat on her back, Lilly drew back and placed both palms on Yasmine's face, thumbing away the tears.

"I know you have a lot on your mind, baby," she said, and again Yasmine felt tears.

"Enough with the waterworks, you're going to look like Morgan Freeman if you don't stop!" The crazy comparison made Yasmine laugh through the tears.

"Morgan Freeman?" she sputtered, once her laughter had died out.

Lilly shrugged. "It's the best I could come up with. You're making me upset with all of this crying. Those big eyes work for him…but on you?" she shook her head, her eyes twinkling. "Not so much."

"No, I guess it wouldn't," Yasmine said, still giggling and sniffing away at the tears.

Lilly patted her hair. "Actually I'm the one who looks more like Morgan than you do, with all of this gray hair in my head and my tiny little fro."

"Aunt Lilly, stop!" Yasmine laughed outright, the tears long gone. Yasmine had taken her aunt into town earlier that day to get her hair trimmed. With her surgery coming up, she'd wanted an easy-to-maintain style. The one she chose was much shorter than before, and complimentary to her angular face.

"You do *not* look like Morgan Freeman!" Again, Yasmine dissolved into giggles, and this time her aunt joined her.

"And I know you want to look your best tomorrow. What with taking me to the hospital…and spending some alone time with Holt," she said softly, making the last of Yasmine's laughter die out at the mention of his name.

"I don't know what Holt has to do with this. He's only coming along because he's worried about you and he loves you."

"Yes, he does. He'd better." She harrumphed. "I raised that boy from the time he wasn't much older than you." She paused. "I know that all of my boys love me. But we both know that's not the only reason he's coming." She turned Yasmine around, forcing her to look at her face. "And you know that as much as I do. He cares about you, too."

"Oh, yeah? Well he sure has a funny way of showing it," she said, shaking her head. "All those women—"

"Those women don't mean a thing to Holt," Lilly cut in, shaking her head. "They never have. They've just filled a void for him. No more, no less."

"Maybe that's all I do for him. Fill a void."

"How do you feel about him?" Lilly turned the tables on her and Yasmine blew out a breath.

Suddenly restless, she rose from the bed and paced the room. "God, I wish I knew, Aunt Lilly."

"Yas, you *do* know." When Yasmine glanced at her aunt, she raised a brow. "Of course I know. You've been carrying a torch for that boy for years. And I know you still care about him. I know that's the reason why you would rarely come back home, unless you knew Holt wasn't around."

Of course Yasmine knew that her aunt was aware of her crush. Although she never spoke about it with her directly, she and Lilly were too close for her to hide her feelings.

"In a way, I was hoping you would have outgrown that. I didn't want to see you hurt. Like I said, the women Holt hung around…" She stopped and shook her head. "He wasn't ready for anything more than what he was able to give them. Then."

"So what makes you think he's any different now?"

Lilly shrugged. "I've watched him grow. Mature. And I have never seen him look at another woman, act the way he has been for the last three weeks because of a woman, as I've seen him with you."

At that Yasmine spun around and stared at her aunt.

"Honey, a blind man can see what's going on with you two. Half the ranch hands tiptoe around Holt, afraid to look at you for fear he'll rip into 'em. You've got the man going in circles." She laughed and patted the bed, inviting Yasmine to sit down next to her.

"If he was all that hot for me, he wouldn't be avoiding me like he has," she said glumly.

"This is all new for him as well, Yas. The thing you two need is to simply sit down and talk. Really talk. About everything. Get it all out." She ran a hand over Yasmine's hair. "You'd be surprised what that will accomplish."

Yasmine shook her head. "But I doubt that'll happen anytime soon. Every time we try we end up arguing or in…" Yasmine stopped, thinking of last night. He'd come home from working and without a word taken her by the hand and led her to his bedroom, and they hadn't come back out for the rest of the night.

Lilly cleared her throat and Yasmine's blush heated her entire face. "I know you have a lot of decisions weighing heavy on you. And with your talents and ambition, the world is yours, baby. And whatever you decide to do, both in your career and your personal life, I'll be here for you."

Yasmine laid her head against her aunt's shoulder and sighed.

Lilly was right. Whether she and Holt ended up together, or simply enjoyed each other for as long as they had, the time was long overdue for the two of them to talk.

Chapter 16

"Aunt Lilly, are you sure you're okay? You don't need anything?" Yasmine asked as she busied herself, bustling around her aunt's hospital room, plumping her pillows. Again. For the fourth time.

"Like I told you the last five times, I'm fine! Now go!" Lilly moved away just in time before Yasmine smacked her with a pillow with her energetic plumping.

Seeing she'd barely missed her aunt's face, she grimaced. "Sorry about that," she mumbled. When Lilly raised a brow, she sheepishly placed the pillow next to her on the narrow bed.

Yasmine focused her attention on Lilly, watching as she situated herself in the bed.

It was early evening, and Lilly had woken from the anesthesia hours ago, with no complications.

The surgery had gone as predicted, smoothly, and her recovery was already well under way. Instead of the typical knee-joint replacement surgery, Lilly had had a less invasive approach, one that promised to lessen the pain of recovery as well as the length of the incision site, which meant less scar tissue for her as she recovered.

However, although Sheridan Memorial was one of the top orthopedic hospitals around, there hadn't been a doctor on staff to perform the new technique, so the brothers had, at their own expense, flown the specialist in.

Although the surgeon was one of the best in his field, Yasmine had been a mass of nerves as she'd sat in the waiting room with Holt, holding his hand tightly. He'd only occasionally left her side, to get coffee, but quickly.

Not until the attending physician had come to the waiting room to tell them of the surgery's success had Yasmine finally relaxed. As they wheeled Lilly into her private room, groggy from the sedation, Yasmine and Holt had been there, waiting.

"Can we get you anything else, Lilly...or do you just want to rest?" Holt broke in, coming to stand by Lilly's bedside.

"I'm fine. You two have done more than enough," she murmured, her voice growing noticeably lower. She waved a weak hand toward Yasmine as she lay back against her pillow. "Take my niece and you two go on back to the hotel. She looks as rough as I feel."

The last words were barely coherent, and Yasmine knew the morphine drip was starting to take its effect.

Within a minute of her speaking, her head rolled to the side, and moments later she was softly snoring.

Yasmine turned to Holt. "You go on back to the hotel. I'll just sit here and wait for her to wake up," she said softly, not wanting to wake Lilly. Although with the amount of pain medication and sedatives being pumped into her system, that and the distinct smile of contentment on her face as she fell into sleep, Yasmine doubted anything could wake her aunt at that point.

She ran a hand over Lilly's hair. She'd been so worried.

She felt Holt's hand on her shoulder and she turned toward him.

"Come on, baby. Let her get some sleep. And she was right, you look just as tired as she does," he admonished, tugging at her until she reluctantly moved away.

"I believe she said I looked rough."

Holt leaned down and placed a soft kiss on her mouth. "You couldn't look rough on your worst day," he murmured against her mouth, and Yasmine leaned into his embrace.

The nurse walked into the room at that moment and informed them that visiting hours were over.

"Guess that's our cue." With that, Holt gently herded Yasmine out of the room. When she stopped once more to look back at her softly dozing aunt, he placed his arm around her waist, drawing her closer. "Don't worry, baby. We'll be back early tomorrow. This way both you and Lilly will be rested. Let's go back to the hotel."

With a nod, she allowed him to lead her away.

They'd arrived in Sheridan early Friday morning, and before going to check in at the hospital had gone to Lilly's preoperative surgery appointment. After filling out all the necessary documents, they'd left after Yasmine had all of her questions answered to her satisfaction.

While her aunt seemed to not show any visible signs of worry about the surgery, Yasmine had been a mass of nerves. And now she was simply glad that it was over.

Lilly had stayed in the hospital that first night, due to the early-morning schedule, and the administrative staff had allowed Yasmine to stay with her. Although Holt had booked two rooms, neither she nor Lilly had used them.

Now, as they were heading back to the hotel, she wondered if he expected her to stay with him in his room, or if he had kept the arrangements the same.

The decision was taken from her when they arrived. Going to the room she and her aunt were supposed to share, she paused at the door, turning to him. "I'll meet you downstairs for dinner later. I think I'm going to go and get some sleep."

"I had your things, as well as Lilly's, moved to my room."

"Why did you do that?"

"When Lilly gets out of the hospital, we'll head back to the ranch. No need for two rooms."

She didn't bother with the argument that *she* still needed a room; it was obvious he'd already made the decision that she'd be staying with him.

"I hope you have two beds."

Yasmine ignored his responding low, throaty laugh.

Holt walked behind Yasmine after opening the door to the room, allowing her to enter first, his eyes trained on the sexy sway of her hips as she strode into the room.

For all that he wanted to pick her up and throw her on the bed and make love to her, the look in her eyes told him that she wasn't ready for that.

He saw her look toward the single king-size bed before her glance shifted to his, the look in her eyes wary, affirming his belief. Although they'd made love again after their first night, her uncertainty showed.

Wanting to put her at ease, he casually nodded toward the bathroom. "Why don't you go and take a nice hot shower. I'm sure it'll help relax you. While you're doing that, I'll go downstairs and scout out the best restaurants in the area. You've got to be hungry," he half asked, and at her nod and hesitant smile, he continued. "Good. I'll find out the where the nearest place is. Sound good?" A relieved smiled lit her face, the dimple in her cheek flashing.

"Why don't you meet me downstairs in, say, oh, thirty minutes?" he asked, and she nodded her head in agreement. Turning to leave, he hesitated at the door, his hand on the knob, and turned back around to face her.

"Yasmine, you don't have anything to worry about, with Lilly. She's going to be fine."

"I know," she said softly. "And thank you for bringing us here. Thank you all for the special care you've made sure Aunt Lilly has. I—" She bit her lip, tugging the full rim into her mouth, and Holt had to close his eyes against the fragile picture she presented, and the way it made him feel.

The way *she* made him feel.

No woman had ever had the ability to do to him with just one look what Yasmine could.

Although tired shadows underscored her eyes, making them appear larger than they were, and her clothes were wrinkled, all traces of makeup gone from her face, she looked more beautiful to him than any one of the scores of models, actresses and socialites he'd dated in the past.

As they stared at each other from across the room, an invisible thread of need, want, desire…and something more, connected them, making it impossible for Holt to look away, to walk the hell away while his intentions remained good. He saw the minute she felt the wild need in him to have her. Her eyes widened, and her chest rose and fell swiftly. But it was her eyes…in her eyes was an answering need, just as wild, mirrored in their dark depths.

They didn't speak; they didn't have to.

"Holt." She whispered his name, her hand coming out in entreaty before dropping at her side.

He drew in a ragged breath. "I'll see you in thirty minutes," he said gruffly, and turned to walk out of the door.

Yasmine lay in bed, staring up at the ceiling, before finally she gave up on sleep.

Glancing at the illuminated numbers on the bedside alarm clock, she blew out a breath in disgust.

It was almost midnight and she was as wide-awake as though she'd had a full night's sleep.

She turned, restless in bed, and grabbed the pillow near her, hugging it close against her chest.

Dinner with Holt had come as a complete surprise. Not sure what to expect after his heavy-handed way of putting them in the same room, as well as the sexual tension between them so thick she could cut it with a knife, she'd been on edge, nervous, yet a part of her was filled with anticipation, wondering what would happen after dinner.

The conversation between them had flowed easily, reminding her of their time when he'd picked her up from the airport. The topics had ranged from their childhood to adulthood, favorite movies and books.

When she sheepishly admitted to being addicted to one of her favorite vampire series on HBO, the two had gone on to argue which character they thought would die by the end of the season and which would finally get what was coming his way.

During the ride up in the elevator, the sexual tension returned, and Yasmine's nerves were on edge. Not because she was afraid of what he'd try, but because she was looking forward to whatever he had in store for her.

When they'd entered the room she'd turned toward him.

"Come here," he said, his voice pitched low.

Yasmine walked toward him, meeting him in the middle of the room.

Holt reached out and wrapped his arms around her waist, bringing her flush against him. Her breath caught when she felt the hard length of his cock press insistently against her stomach.

"You look beat. Why don't you get some rest?" he said, pulling away from her, running his eyes over her face. "I'm going to head back down to the bar and grab a couple of beers, maybe catch the game. I'll be quiet when I come back up, you won't even know I'm here," he promised, and with a kiss on her forehead left her with her mouth hanging open, wondering what in the world had just happened.

Going downstairs to have a beer and watch a football game?

Her brow furrowed in the dark. She was by no means what you would call a sports enthusiast, but even *she* knew football season hadn't started, she thought, her confusion growing. She'd definitely given him enough signals over dinner that she was…interested in a repeat of what they'd shared.

So what happened? What did she do?

Maybe he'd already gotten tired of her and was ready to move on to the next conquest.

She turned over in bed, irritated, confused…and horny, and hugged the pillow even tighter as she mentally counted sheep, dogs, cats…whatever, in an attempt to force the mindlessness that came with sleep to overtake her and force her to stop thinking of Holt.

Holt eased inside the room, quietly closing the door behind him. The room was quiet and completely dark, and as he made his way farther in, he glanced toward the bed. Not wanting to wake Yasmine, he sat down in the chair and eased off his shoes and socks, leaving his feet bare, then walked over to where she lay.

In the dark he could barely make out her form as she lay on her side, tightly hugging the pillow close to her body. She'd kicked off the sheet so that it only covered one half of her body. Her pretty rear end was raised, the ends of her silky-looking gown just barely covering her round, plush bottom. She moved, shifting the sheet away even more, exposing even more.

Reaching out a hand, he went to touch her and drew back when she softly snored, snorted and shoved her face deeper into the pillow.

So much for her waiting up for him, he thought with an inner sigh.

It was his own damn fault.

He forced himself to move away from the temptation she presented and went into the bathroom instead. He closed the door, shed his clothes and turned on the shower.

The room he'd chosen was a large suite, and the bathroom was located far enough from the bedroom area that he knew the sound wouldn't wake her.

He stepped inside the shower and immediately turned his face into the stinging spray.

It had been pure hell leaving her earlier. And he knew that it wouldn't have taken much persuasion for him to have her naked and under his body, calling his name as he stroked deep inside her, giving them both what they wanted, what they needed.

The memory of how good she felt wrapped around him, the way her walls clung to him perfectly, the way she moved her hips until neither one of them could walk the next day.

But she'd looked so damn vulnerable, the strain of the day showing on her face.

He grabbed the bar of soap and quickly lathered it over his body, thinking he should have turned the water to cold, anything to make the images of her and what he wanted to do to her sinfully delicious body go the hell away.

Chapter 17

Yasmine woke up out of a light sleep when she heard the shower come on.

She turned toward the clock again, and saw that somehow she must have managed to get some sleep, the illuminated numbers telling her it was almost 1:00 a.m.

She plopped back down on the bed, lost in thought.

Her sleep had been fractured at best, as even in her dreams Holt refused to go away.

She could either lie in bed and try and pretend her body wasn't on fire, in need of his touch, or she could do something about it.

She made a decision and left the bed.

She was going to do something about it. Her bare feet sank into the plush carpeting as she crossed over to the bathroom. Before she could lose her nerve, she turned the knob and walked inside.

She came to a standstill just inside the door when she saw his silhouetted form in the shower and her feet carried her as though with a will of their own.

His face was directly in the spray, the water sluicing off his hair and skin, running down over his big body.

Unable to look away, she watched as he grabbed the bar of soap. After getting a good lather, he ran his soapy hands over his body, down his chest and thighs, before he grasped his shaft.

She swallowed, her gaze fixed on his hand, big, cupped around his straining shaft.

He ran his hand over the length of his cock, root to stem, the movements slow, methodical.

He hesitated and the speed of his hand movement gliding along his cock quickened, the motion becoming shorter, faster.

Yasmine felt her body respond to the way he was touching himself. She imagined it was her hand running along the thick ridge, her hand lightly touching the mushroom cap…her tongue…

Holt raised his eyes and met Yasmine's.

Slowly, keeping his gaze on hers, he casually removed his hand from his cock and turned off the water.

He opened the glass door and stepped out, not bothering to grab the towel draped over the bar to cover himself as he walked toward her.

Her glance fell to his naked shaft, jutting out thick, male. Eager.

She slowly dragged her passion-glazed eyes to meet his.

"Touch it," he dared her, and her eyes flew to his as her tongue snaked out to moisten her dry lips.

"I…I'd better go," she said, and he caught her before she spun around. "I'm sorry, I shouldn't have—"

"It's not like you haven't seen it before," he murmured, his words making her stop.

Her heart raced and her nipples beaded against her silk gown when she felt him approach her.

"You know you want to." His warm breath fanned the side of her head as he bent close to whisper the words.

Yasmine swallowed.

"Go ahead. Touch it." The words were a dark challenge, as though he knew she wouldn't do it. He placed his hands on the tops of her shoulders, moving her body so that she faced him.

She licked her tongue over her mouth a second time, her eyes drawn again to his shaft.

Thick, long, it was flushed a dark rose, straining.

She glanced up at him. The ends of his nostrils were flared, the look of carnal lust brightening his eyes, yet he didn't move. Didn't take her hand and place it over that part of him she desperately wanted to feel. To taste. To touch.

She swallowed. Hesitantly her hand reached for him, taking him in her palm and stroking over the velvet skin of his shaft.

She heard his groan, but continued her soft caress. Her fingers danced over his entire length, tracing over the deep vein that pulsed beneath her fingertips from his base, where his sac tightly nestled against his shaft, to the mushroom tip, and she ran a finger over the small eye, wiping away at the bead of moisture.

"You're beautiful." The words escaped without conscious thought.

"Yasmine." He choked out her name. Seeing the look on his face, the way her touch was affecting him, gave her a surge of feminine power. For her to have such an effect on him was a heady feeling.

She kept her eyes on his as she leaned toward him, planting a kiss over his male nipple. Although she wasn't experienced in making the first moves, instinct took over, and she mimicked what he'd done to her when they made love.

Her tongue darted out to stroke and lick the nub, drawing it deeply into her mouth and suckling him, much as he'd done to her.

As she kissed and laved him, her hand closed around his shaft, her fingers barely able to circle him. She continued her teasing touches, her hand running up and over his rock-hard shaft.

With a final lick, she ran her tongue down his chest.

"What are you doing?" he rasped, and placed his hand at the back of her head, anchoring her to his chest.

Continuing her path she followed the line of hair in the center of his body, stopping when she came to his belly button. Bending slightly to better reach him, she struck her tongue inside, smiling against his stomach when she felt his low goan.

The hand in her hair clenched, tightening when her tongue went lower.

"Enough," he bit out, forcing her to stand.

He lifted her, placing his hands beneath her bottom, and sat her on the bathroom counter. Before she could protest, if she was of a mind to, he had her panties off and on the floor. Crouched low, he glanced up at her.

Slowly, his big hands grasped her by both of her ankles, moving up, past her knees, until they rested on her thighs. Keeping his eyes on hers, he parted her thighs, moved in closer.

She held her breath when his head moved in, expelling on a long breath when she felt the tip of his tongue against her inner thigh, the brush of his mouth against her mound.

"Mmm," she sighed, releasing the breath slowly, her hands planted on the counter on either side of her.

His fingers dug into her hips as he angled her so that her mound rested firmly against his mouth.

She felt his breath fan against the hairs covering her, and she screamed when he stroked between her crease with one long sweep of his tongue.

With each stroke, he carefully avoided her quivering bud, swirling his tongue around it, beside it, but not taking it inside his mouth. He took his time with her. Savored her as though she were his last meal.

Yasmine glanced down, moaning, her body on fire;

the sight of his dark blond head between her thighs, the feel of him catering to her, was too much. As much as she wanted him to continue his sensual torture, she didn't know that she could accept much more.

"Oh God, Holt, baby...please...Holt, slow down. I—" Her protest ended on a sharp cry of disbelief when he brought her straining nub into his mouth and bit down lightly on it.

She felt the erotic sting of his kiss all the way to her toes, and her spine arched, her head falling back, as he continued his teasing strokes.

He finally drew her bud deep into his mouth; tugging gently on it, he gave her what she desperately needed.

When her orgasm hit, she grabbed his head, pulling him closer, and screamed her release.

"I can't wait, baby. I'm sorry, I've got to have you." She heard Holt speak as though from a distance, her body completely boneless. She barely had enough strength to place her hands around his neck when he lifted her from the counter.

She nodded her head weakly against his hard chest, too spent to speak as he carried her out of the bathroom and laid her on the bed.

He reached over, fumbled in the bedside table and withdrew a package before he joined her on the bed. Then he was on the bed, positioning her body so that he lay directly behind her.

"I need you, baby. I need you now." He growled the words against her neck. "Please tell me you need me, too," he begged huskily. He reached around her, his fingers delving between her legs, finding her core and testing her readiness for him, his fingers coming away with proof that she was.

She heard a rip behind her, the rustling of movement and jostling of her body before moments later, she felt the tip of his shaft as he slowly penetrated her from the back.

In one long, hot glide, Holt pushed inside Yasmine's body, pressing past the slight resistance until he was fully seated.

Once he was all the way in, he stopped, resting his head against the curve of her neck. Her walls clamped so tightly on him he had to grit his teeth and force himself not to move for fear he'd release too soon.

God, she felt so good wrapped around him.

So right.

He held the position for as long as he could.

"Are you ready for me?" He breathed the words against her neck.

She nodded her head, glancing over her shoulder at him.

The light from the bathroom cast a sensual glow over her face, the look in her eyes as she stared at him one of lust, desire…and something more.

He swallowed deeply, gritting his teeth as he felt his shaft grow even harder wedged deep inside her body.

Closing his eyes, he tightened his jaw, his mind fighting against what she made him feel with just one look.

The only thought on his mind was making love to

her. For as long as they had together, he intended to love her as no man ever had, or ever would.

She looked back over her shoulder, the expression on her face a combination of virginal innocence mixed with sultry seductiveness. "What are you waiting for?" she asked, her voice low, throaty.

With a growl, Holt tightened his hold on her and shifted his hips, drawing himself nearly out of her before gliding back in.

Her mewling echoed in the room.

The feel of her walls clamping down on him, molding and adjusting to his length and girth, sent an electric shock of pleasure through his body.

She was his. For as long as he had her, as long as she was at Wyoming Wilde, she belonged to him.

His hands shook as they gripped her hips tighter, plunging into her softness, his pace and depth of stroke quickening as she bucked back against him, grinding her body against his shaft, accepting his body, molding and adjusting to his, as though she'd been made just for him.

With every plunge of his body, she gave back as much, until their seesawing motion began to rock the bed.

She felt so tight, so good wrapped around him, her walls milking him as he delved into her, over and over. Her firm globes slapped in a rhythmic beat against his stomach, her mewling cries growing with every glide and retreat.

A roll of her hips against his body was his undoing.

He felt the beginnings of an orgasm, but he held on. Sweat dripped down from his chest to land on her back.

She arched, slowly, sensually, as though she felt even that smallest of nuances.

God, she was so responsive to him.

Gritting his teeth, Holt lifted her by the waist, rose and moved one of his bent knees so that one foot was flat on the mattress and continued to thrust, realigning their bodies so that with every downward plunge the top of his shaft scraped her straining clitoris.

"Oh, oh, oh, oh…." she panted, her voice hoarse. "Holt, baby…Holt, Holt, Holt, Holt, Holt." She cried out his name, blurring it together as though it were some erotic prayer, over and over, until he felt her body stiffen, her spine arch.

"I'm coming, baby, I—" Her words ended in a scream when he reached between their joined bodies, found her hot nub and pinched. With one last thrust he sent them both over into oblivion, their cries of release echoing, bouncing off the walls, melding into one harmonious cry of satisfaction.

"I remember the first day you came to the ranch."

It was several minutes before Yasmine could muster enough energy to speak. Her body limp, she'd collapsed onto the mattress after her tumultuous release.

She opened drowsy eyes, found herself lying on Holt's chest and smiled. She didn't know the last time she'd felt so…relaxed.

"Oh, you do, do you?" she asked, her voice husky. She cleared her throat, blushing when she realized her voice was so scratchy from all of her yelling. "And what do you remember?"

Although she lay on top of him and was unable to see his face, Yasmine heard the smile come through in Holt's voice.

"I remember you were wearing a really fancy-looking little dress, complete with black shiny shoes and a hat." He laughed and she groaned, remembering the outfit and how out of place she'd felt when she'd arrived at the ranch dressed up, the only girl on the ranch filled with men and boys in dirty jeans. She wrinkled her nose.

"I can't believe you remember that!"

"I do. But mostly I remember the hat. It was pretty," he said, startling a laugh out of her. "I had never seen a hat like that. If you tell my brothers that, I swear I'll hunt you down," he said, laughing with her.

"I won't," she promised. "Scout's honor." She held up two fingers, making the vow official.

"I remember that day, as well. I remember mostly how afraid I was during the plane trip over." A reminiscent smile lifted the corners of her mouth. "We flew over the Teton Mountains. And I remember looking down and everything looking so different than what I was used to. When Aunt Lilly came to get me at the airport I remember the ride back and only seeing mountains, flatlands and bush." She laughed. "She thought I was quiet because I was shy. I was just taking it all in." She smiled in memory.

"I bet it was a lot for a little girl to take in," he said, running a hand over her hair.

"It was. Everything was just so much more...quiet than what I was used to, living in New York. No tall buildings obscured the sky, like we had back home, nothing but mountains was all I could see. No taxis honking at you to get out of the way, and everybody spoke English," she said, and heard his quiet laughter.

"And then you fell in love with it," he said softly, and Yasmine smiled. Although he was referring to the ranch, she knew she'd also started to fall in love with him a little that day.

"Yeah, I did. It was scary at first, I didn't know what to do, how to act. Who to be," she said, her voice losing some of its faraway note. "But, between Aunt Lilly, Jed... and of course, you, Nate and Shilah, I felt welcomed." She stopped and laughed, the sound bittersweet. "In fact I felt more at home at Wyoming Wilde than I'd ever felt with my parents. I think that's what I felt the most guilt about, after they died."

He hugged her close. "It was understandable, with them traveling so much, and you staying with relatives most of the time. That doesn't mean you didn't love them." He hugged her, and she turned into his embrace.

Yasmine knew that Holt, as well as his brothers, knew what her life had been like before she'd come to live with him. She remembered the night she'd come to stay with them. Not being able to sleep, she'd crept downstairs quietly to pour herself a glass of milk.

Before she'd walked into the kitchen she heard voices and stopped, crouching against the wall, and listened when she heard her name mentioned by Jed Wilde, the man her aunt worked for, and father of the three boys she'd met earlier that day.

Jed had been in the process of explaining to the boys that she was going to be living with them, and that her parents had just died. Yasmine had kept her body low, listening as the young boys had plied Jed with questions, asking where she was from, what happened to her parents and how long she'd be living with them.

When she'd met Jed earlier that day, she'd been more than a little bit intimidated by him. Tall, he had to be the tallest man she'd ever seen, with a voice so deep her eyes had widened into saucers when she heard him speak.

Yet despite his gruff manner, he answered his boys' questions patiently, and after he'd answered them had told the boys that Yasmine was now family. Just like them, she was family.

She'd peeked around the corner and saw them each nod their heads solemnly. Nate, who she'd guessed was the oldest, spoke first. "You can count on us, Dad. We'll make sure she feels at home," he'd said, his voice breaking in the middle of his sentence, in that way boys had when their voices were about to change and deepen.

"She'll be family." Shilah spoke then. Yasmine had been fascinated by the middle brother, the way his dark solemn eyes had watched her closely when they had met earlier in the day. Not saying a word, he'd simply stuck out his hand for her to shake.

But it had been Holt whom Yasmine believed she fell a little bit in love with that night when he piped in, volunteering his room for her to stay in. Jed had laughed gruffly, assuring his youngest son that they had more than enough room for Yasmine, that she'd stay in the new room they'd added to the upstairs wing.

Although so uniquely different on the outside, Nate being black, Holt white and Shilah Native American, on the inside the boys were as similar as if the same blood ran in their veins. Jed had a lot to do with forming them into the young men that they became.

As Yasmine remembered that year she'd come to live with them, the dark room, Holt's strong arms wrapped around her waist, holding her close as she lay on him, all gave her the freedom to speak what she'd held on to for a long time.

The words seemed to pour out of her: how afraid she'd been, how even though she loved her parents, she hadn't been able to cry at their funeral. She felt nothing but anger, anger that they left her and even more anger that they hadn't taken her with them when they decided to take a vacation.

Anger that they'd left her alone.

"I guess I was most angry because I never felt like my parents even knew I existed. They were always traveling, and they always left me behind. When I'd ask…beg… them to take me, I can remember my mother telling me they were going to do 'grown-up fun' and promising that one day soon, when I was older, we'd all go on a trip together.

"It wasn't until I came to live at the ranch that I felt…" She stopped and drew in a breath. "That I felt like I really had a home. With people who loved me. I didn't have to feel alone anymore. I had a family."

When he released her, she laid her head back on his chest. Saying aloud what she'd kept deep inside for years was freeing. She felt a burden she hadn't been aware she'd been carrying lift from her shoulders.

"And now? Have you found that same sense of contentment in your life you found with us…with your aunt, when you lived at the ranch?"

The question momentarily caught her off guard. She frowned, thinking of the places she'd traveled, all over the world, and the accomplishments she'd made. For all of her achievements, there was a part of her that still yearned for the sense of home she'd only felt at Wyoming Wilde.

"I don't know," she said softly.

The uncertainty, but mostly the honesty in her voice, reached out and when he least expected it sucker punched Holt directly in his heart.

She was so open, so giving.

He felt humbled at the way she opened up to him, told him things she'd never mentioned to anyone else.

Humbled and ashamed.

Ashamed because he hadn't been able to do the same.

As he'd listened to her, he'd heard the sadness in her

voice when she spoke about her parents. The loneliness she felt even when they were home, and how even then she felt separate from them, as though they were in their own world, one she didn't share with them.

So much of what she said, he felt deep inside. He'd wanted to open up to her, as well. Wanted to tell her how he could relate to much of what she said, that he, too, knew what it felt like to be alone, even if he was in a crowded room.

But the thought of exposing himself to her, to anyone, in that way, in a way he never had before, even with his brothers, wasn't something he was willing to do. To see sympathy in her eyes, like he'd seen so many times in the past when he was younger... No, he wanted no one's sympathy. Not even Yasmine's.

He hugged her close, showing in action what he couldn't say in words.

He could get used to this...to her. Waking up to her every day, her warm body close to his, their bodies aching from a night spent loving each other.

He mentally brought himself up short. Not loving. Sex. Having sex with each other. Lovers for the rest of her stay at the ranch.

And how will you feel once she's gone? an inner voice asked.

He settled against her. He'd cross that bridge when he came to it. For now, this was all he needed. All he had to give.

As her head lay on his chest, Holt ran a hand over

her hair. He loved the way the thick strands felt against his fingers.

He was still thinking of the things she had shared with him, along with his own mixed-up feelings, long after he heard her soft snores telling him she'd gone to sleep.

Chapter 18

"I was thinking. When we get back to the ranch, how would you feel about moving in with me?"

"What are you talking about? I'm already staying at the ranch," Yasmine said, frowning up at him.

"No, I meant into my room."

"Are you joking? God, Holt, Aunt Lilly would kill us both!" She laughed off the suggestion. Although a part of her found the idea appealing, she didn't want to even think what her aunt would have to say about it.

It was late, and in less than six hours they would be heading back to the hospital to pick Lilly up and return to the ranch.

Over the past three days when they weren't spending time with Lilly, and Holt wasn't on the phone with his brothers, they were with one another, going into downtown Sheridan at night. Although it was still early spring, and the nighttime air could grow cold, they enjoyed walking around the picturesque part of town, mostly window shopping, as many of the shops had closed by the time they reached the area.

Their time together had seemed so idyllic, almost standing outside time. A part of Yasmine wished she could capture the moments and lock them away, storing them to savor for the time when she would have to leave. And after hearing from Lilly's doctors, she knew that before long her aunt would be up and around and wouldn't need Yasmine's help.

They'd been surprised when they'd gone to see her the day after the surgery and she was up walking around, with the help of a cane. As the doctors had taken a less invasive approach to Lilly's knee-joint replacement, her recovery, they'd been told, would be half the time of a normal knee surgery, a fact that relieved Yasmine. Her expected recovery time would be no more than a few weeks.

When Yasmine realized how quickly her aunt would recover, although she was happy for Lilly, a part of her was saddened, knowing her time at Wyoming Wilde would soon be coming to an end.

"And you don't think she'll figure out that we're sleeping together when we get back?" he asked, bringing her back to the subject at hand. He cupped one of her cheeks in his hand and squeezed, making her squirm. "That *everyone* won't figure it out?" he asked, and she blushed.

"Humph!" she said, lying half on top of his body and propping her chin on his chest. "You say that as though this is going to continue."

"If by 'this,' you mean this…" He stopped and tugged her so that she lay full on top of him. He brought their lips together, ran his tongue over her mouth and kissed her slowly.

"And this…" he murmured against her mouth once he released it, placed a hand on her hip and lightly ground her against his hardening shaft. "Then, yes, I would say I have every intention on continuing."

"I don't know, Holt. Things are pretty busy for me, and for you as well, with breeding season and the auction coming up. Maybe you won't have time for me," she said coyly when he finally released her, hiding her smile.

"Are you kidding me?" he asked feigning disbelief. "You must not know who I am. I always schedule time for my ladies for hot juicy sex."

"Hot juicy sex?" she said, her voice rising another octave. "Your ladies? Is that all I am to you, Holt?"

As soon as he said it, she could tell he wished he could bite out his own tongue.

"Is that all I am to you, just another notch on your belt, another one of your ladies to give you all that hot juicy sex you need?"

"Oh God, Yas, I was just kidding! I didn't mean it like that!"

"Whatever, Holt," she said, and pushed him away angrily when he tried to bring her back to his side. "That's your problem. Everything is a joke to you." She rose and gathered her clothes, angrily jerking her arms through her bra, missing the snaps. Finally giving up, she drew her blouse over her head.

"Obviously, so am I."

"What are you doing, Yas?" he asked, his face bewildered. "Aww, baby, don't be like that. Come on back. I was just—"

"You know what? Just stop. Stop playing…the Penthouse! That act is getting real old, real fast."

The cajoling expression slipped from his features as his eyes narrowed into slits.

"Yasmine, I told you not to call me that before."

"And if I do?"

She glanced back at him and ignored her body's reaction to the sexy image he presented on the bed, lying sprawled out, half-naked, the sheet barely covering his…essentials.

"No, Holt. I know *exactly* who you are. You're just a little boy who's afraid of growing up," she said quietly, turning away from him. "And I'm tired of trying to figure you out. Just leave me alone. Please." She ran toward the door and placed her hand on the knob before he was there, placing his hand over hers.

"I'll get another room…or wait in the lobby until it's time to go and see Aunt Lilly at the hospital. Either way, I'm out."

"Don't go. Please," he said, his voice husky. "I'm sorry."

She said nothing, keeping her hand on the door.

"Just come back to bed. Please. I'm sorry. What I said was stupid."

She turned her head away, not quite ready to forgive him.

"We have a few more hours before we can go to see Lilly. I can think of a lot more interesting things we can do besides argue."

She looked up at him, ready to head out of the door, when she paused, her eyes searching his.

Although his words were light, casual, in his eyes she read something different entirely. What she saw was fear, fear of allowing her in, past the last barrier he'd erected between himself and the world.

What she read made her realize that she wasn't ready to give up on him, on them, on what they could have, if only he let her in.

She drew her hand away from the knob and placed it in his, allowing him to lead her back to bed, and his arms.

Chapter 19

Yasmine glanced at the clock, checking to see how much time she had before Holt would be home for dinner. After helping Jackie load the warming plates to send to the mess hall for the others, she'd gone back to preparing their meal.

Tonight they were going to eat together, just the two of them, and later go dancing.

The thought of getting away from the ranch for some alone time with Holt and going dancing with him had kept her excited all day. With breeding season upon them, the past couple of weeks they'd barely managed to see each other during the day.

That, as well as the time she'd spent with Lilly, planning the final menu for Althea and Nate's wedding, and her own duties, and the two of them had managed to spend time together only at night.

Occasionally she wondered if he longed for her in the way she longed for him. Even when they were apart, thoughts of Holt were never far from her mind. She also wondered if he'd ever trust her enough to allow her to get past that last barrier, the invisible one he kept between himself and the rest of the world.

Whenever doubts surfaced she brushed them away for the time being, and forced herself to enjoy the moment, and the time they had left together.

Not that it all had been idyllic. It was getting harder and harder for Yasmine to keep her love for him quiet, especially during lovemaking. She wondered what his feelings were for her.

Behind the jokes and sometimes irreverent sense of humor he showed, at times Yasmine saw the cracks behind the mask he presented to the world.

When he took her out to the cottage where he and his brothers, along with their foster father, had once lived, she'd gotten a view, although only briefly, of the part of himself, his personality, he kept firmly locked away.

When he thought she wasn't looking, she'd catch a strange expression crossing his handsome face. She felt at those times like a specimen under his own private microscope.

Maybe he was trying to figure her out, just as she was him. She didn't know. There was still so much about him she hadn't figured out, she thought as she absently stirred the pot.

Enjoy the moment. Which she was doing with fervor. Although both of them were busy, too busy during the day to spend any real time together, Holt more than made up for their time spent apart at night, she thought, a feminine smile tugging at her mouth as she remembered last night.

He'd come home earlier than usual, and after a hasty dinner where he'd barely allowed her to say good-night to her aunt, he'd hustled her to his room, where he promptly showed her just how much he missed her.

And throwing herself completely into their love-making, she returned the favor.

Yasmine paused in her thinking, her hand coming to a stop.

She was in love with Holt.

Not a young girl's crush, but the love only a woman could have for her man.

"You look so at home in the kitchen, Yasmine."

Yasmine whirled around, completely surprised to see Clayton Moore standing in the kitchen hallway. She dropped the spoon she'd been stirring inside the large pot.

"Clayton, what…what are you doing here?"

"Well, if Mohammed won't come to the mountain, I guess the mountain has to come to Mohammed." He quipped the clichéd saying, walking toward her.

He smiled widely, his bleached teeth standing out sharply against his sienna-colored skin.

"You're keeping busy, I see," he said, stopping when he came within arm's distance.

"Oh, uh, yes, I have!" she said, mentally scrambling, trying to figure out why he'd come.

She frowned. "Did I miss something? Did you tell me you were coming?"

"Well, I thought I would surprise you."

"Yes, you have. But why?"

Her oven timer went off before he could answer and she turned away, lifting the heavy, large dish from the oven and placing it on the stove.

She turned back around to face him, the slightest bit irritated that he hadn't bothered trying to help her. At least an offer.

"You look quite at home here," he said, not bothering to answer her question.

Yasmine drew the oven mitts from her hands, slowly placing them on the counter.

"I came because I want you."

"What?" So stunned, Yasmine was nearly speechless with the bald statement.

He laughed, coming closer. "Don't act surprised, Yasmine. I haven't exactly tried to hide that fact."

She backed away from him. "But I thought you wanted me as your executive chef. Not as—"

"My lover?" he asked, raising an arched brow.

As Yasmine listened to him speak, she ran her gaze over him, wondering what she'd ever found attractive about him.

His eyebrows, nails and hair were more manicured than her own, and he exuded an oily charm that suddenly sent shivers over her body.

"Of course I want you for the executive chef…the notoriety you'll bring will make my new restaurant even more successful. But can't I have both?" he asked, his blazing-white teeth flashing as he smiled. Before she could discern his next move, he had her, his arms wrapping around her body and pulling her close.

Surprised, Yasmine didn't move as his warm, moist lips moved over hers.

When his clammy fingers dug into her arms, Yasmine snapped out of her daze and renewed her struggle. Finally she pried his arms away from hers, and shoved at his chest until he stumbled away.

Wiping her mouth with the back of her hand, she kept her gaze on Clayton, eyeing him warily.

From the look on his face, Yasmine knew that he was aware that he'd overstepped his boundaries.

"Yasmine, I'm sorry. I—"

"I think you need to go. Now," she said, anger making her voice tremble.

Before she could finish the thought a voice interrupted.

"Seems like I'm interrupting something."

Holt was standing in the doorway, arms crossed over his big chest. To the casual observer he was relaxed, poised even, as his glance went from Yasmine to Clayton. But, Yasmine saw the muscle twitch in the corner of his mouth, a sure sign that he was barely holding on to his anger.

"Holt, it wasn't—" A hard look crossed his face,

stopped her from speaking. He turned cold eyes her way.

"This is Clayton Moore," she said, desperately trying to get a good gauge on him, wondering how much he'd heard…how much he'd seen. Dread pooled in her gut at the cold look on his face.

"I told you about him…he's just here about the offer."

"I'm sure he is," he said, his lips curling. "I don't want to keep you from your…plans. I've got plans of my own."

Yasmine frowned. "What plans? I thought you and I—?"

He cut in on her. "About that. I have to take a rain check. I was coming to find you to tell you that I got a call from my own…business associate and I won't be able to keep our plans. Maybe next time."

"What the hell? Maybe next time?" Yasmine frowned. "Who is this business associate?" Although she asked, anger began to boil up inside Yasmine after his insinuation sunk in.

Not only did he think she was kissing another man, he had come to tell her he was breaking their date for what she could only gather was another woman.

Before she could say another word, he turned and strode from the room.

"Look, I'm sorry. I didn't mean for that to happen. I can go to him, explain." Clayton stopped when she held out a hand to him. She'd almost forgotten he was there. Turning to him she shook her head.

"Just go. Please." She couldn't look at Clayton, couldn't deal with him, not right now.

"I'm sorry, Yasmine. I really am," he said to her back. She heard his footsteps as he walked down the hall and left the house.

Chapter 20

Yasmine killed the engine to her Camry, grabbed her oversize satchel from the passenger seat and placed it in her lap. Before she withdrew the keys from the ignition, she listened to the melodic lyrics to one of her favorite ballads, as the singer crooned about being half-crazy in love.

She could definitely relate. She had to be half-crazy. What other reason would she be out this late at night buying chocolate-chip-cookie ingredients?

She glanced toward her backseat, seeing the two overflowing bags filled with not only ingredients for cookies, but a carton of milk…couldn't eat cookies without milk, she thought. Along with a gallon of cookie-dough ice cream…well, just because…along with an assortment of other "needed" items.

Yep. Half-crazy. That was her.

She'd gone to the grocery store over an hour ago. Although it was late, she'd decided a batch of chocolate-chip cookies were just what the doctor ordered.

A survey of her pantry and she realized she was missing several key ingredients. Rather than giving up on the notion, unable to sleep, she'd mentally shrugged and made a quick dash to the store.

All in an attempt to keep her mind busy. As though she didn't have enough to think about.

She'd chosen not to accept Clayton's offer, wrestling with her options for weeks before making her final decision.

After everything that had happened, despite Clayton's assurances that it would be strictly professional, Yasmine had decided against taking the position.

Instead, she'd met with the producers of the food network. When they'd told her they would love to do a show based on the ranch and "country cooking" made elegant, she'd felt close to tears. Although she hadn't told them of her change in plans and the show hadn't been finalized yet, she'd accepted the offer.

When she was better able to deal with everything, she'd tell them.

But even the firm offer of her own show hadn't made her feel any better, despite the magnitude of what it would do for her career.

Heartbroken, she'd simply accepted the position, knowing that it would take her career to the next level.

After thanking the neighbor who'd been watering her plants and collecting her mail in her absence, and chatting briefly with the elderly woman, Yasmine had gone to her apartment, eager to check her messages. She hadn't received any calls on her cell from anyone except her aunt, but in the back of her mind, she'd hoped there would be one from Holt on her home phone. Although there were a slew of messages, none had been from Holt.

Although, considering the last time they'd spoken and what had happened, she didn't know why she felt anything for him at all. He had made his thoughts and feelings about her abundantly clear.

The memory alone made her cringe, of the neutral look on his face after she'd caught up with him…the way he looked at her as though she meant nothing to him, not to mention the words he threw out that cut her as deeply as any of her sharp-edged knives ever could.

The rest of the week, she hadn't seen him, and later found out from her aunt that he'd gone to Cheyenne on business regarding the ranch. She doubted he had any business but that he simply didn't want to be around her.

She'd also realized that he didn't think she'd been kissing another man, and neither had he been about to cancel their date. He'd used the situation to get out of their relationship

When he returned, and for the remainder of the two weeks that Yasmine was there, he managed to completely avoid her.

At that point she wanted to be as far away from him as he obviously wanted to be from her, but she couldn't leave. As soon as Lilly was walking around without assistance, Yasmine had decided it was time for her to go. Their farewell had been emotional at best.

She hadn't had to tell her aunt what happened, her reasons for leaving. Lilly, as well as everyone else on the ranch, knew. It was impossible not to.

Before she left, she promised a tearful Althea that she could as easily work on the menu for her wedding from New York as she could from the ranch, and promised to return for the ceremony.

She listened to the last crooning notes play out and the DJ's husky voice break in before she slipped the key from the ignition and opened her door.

After retrieving the bags from the back, she balanced them against one hip and with the other bumped the car door closed, before hurrying up the walk leading to her garden-level apartment.

When she saw someone leaving, opening the door, she hurried her steps, her arms so full with groceries peeking over the tops of the bags, she couldn't see who it was, but hoped they'd see her and keep the door open.

She mumbled a thank-you once she'd walked into the lobby, unable to see whom it was she thanked with her vision obscured with the bags.

"My pleasure," a deep voice answered, and Yasmine nearly dropped the bags.

"Let me help you with that," Holt said, taking the

bags from her and rescuing the carton of milk before it made a nosedive onto the floor.

"What…when…what are you doing here?" she asked, so surprised to see him standing there in the lobby of her apartment building that she could only stare up at him.

He took the rest of her bags from her, his expression solemn. "Can we go inside and talk about that?"

Yasmine briefly hesitated before nodding her head, her heart thumping wildly inside her chest.

She lived on the ground floor, so the walk to her apartment was less than a few feet. She used the time to run a glance over him.

Missing were the usual jeans and chambray work shirt, as well as the Stetson he always wore on the ranch. Instead he wore a pair of dress slacks and a silk shirt, easily slipping into the casual sophistication like the chameleon he was.

She glanced away from him.

The memory of the way he'd casually dismissed her, refused to speak to her, helped her to harden her heart.

Her hands fumbled as she dug inside her bag for her key. With shaky fingers she managed to insert it into the lock and open the door.

Standing back, she allowed him to enter.

"You can put them on the counter," she said, motioning toward the bar-style kitchen counter.

Once he had placed the bags down, he turned, glancing over her small apartment.

"It's small, but it's home," she said, looking at her place through his eyes.

It was the first place she'd called home since leaving the ranch. Until that point, Yasmine had lived in dormitories while in school, or rented small apartments during her apprenticeship.

She'd ripped down the previous renter's dusty pastel wallpaper, and had painted the rooms in muted yet light colors, using the sunshine that streamed in through the windows to enhance the airy feel.

Rent was expensive in New York, and unable to find a one-bedroom within her budget, and not wanting a roommate, she'd rented the studio, using the large open room off the kitchen as both living and bedroom space.

Although it was small, she loved her apartment.

"It's pretty, Yas," he said, and she heard the sincerity in his voice.

She turned back to face him. "Why did you come, Holt? You made your feelings clear the last time we spoke. Did you forget something?"

At that he closed his eyes, briefly, blowing out a long sigh. "Baby, I'm sorry. I didn't mean—"

"Baby?" She shook her head. "You gave up the right to call me that when you thought I was kissing another man and when you calmly waltzed in to tell me you had a date with another woman." She spat the words.

"I'm so sorry, Yas. If I could take back what I said, I would. God, baby, you have to know I didn't mean that. Please," he said.

She pulled away from him. "No. You can't just say whatever the hell you want, ignore me, refuse to talk to me, and think you can just waltz back in my life and tell me you're sorry and I forgive you?" She ended the last word on a question. "I don't know why you're here, but you can go back the way you came. I'm—"

"I love you, Yasmine. Please, baby, don't send me away."

She closed her eyes, fighting back the tears and anger that both warred for dominance.

"You hurt me, Holt." She whispered the words.

She felt his hand on her shoulder, felt him pull her around, forcing her to look at him. The wealth of emotion she saw in his eyes before his mouth descended on hers forced a cry from her lips, even as he covered them with his own.

The kiss seemed to last an eternity. The minute their lips met, Yasmine's body was on fire. She kissed him with all the yearning, anger and betrayal that she had been living with since the day he turned away from her.

He pulled her closer, lifting her in his arms. "Where's your bedroom?" he asked, around her lips. "Please, baby, I've got to feel you, know that you're still mine."

She closed her eyes and nodded toward the living area. "One and same," she said, barely able to get the words out.

He carried her to the large sofa sleeper that occupied the corner of the room. Before he laid her down on the soft cushions, he had her shirt up and over her head, her sweats along with her panties soon joining them on the floor.

Quickly divesting himself of his own clothing, he was hot, naked and hard, his body crushing hers into the cushions.

He devoured her lips, his tongue greedily reaching within her mouth and stroking along hers. Yasmine's moans turned to a sharply indrawn breath when she felt the hand that had inserted itself between them reach the V of her legs and push past her entry, testing her readiness for him.

"I don't know how long this is going to last, Yas. I'm so hungry for you… Baby, I missed you so much," he said, his words muffled against the corner of her mouth. Yasmine cried out when his finger pressed farther inside. When he felt her essence cover his fingers, he groaned against the side of her neck.

She desperately clung to his mouth, her hands scoring his back as she pulled him tighter against her.

"It's okay…" she panted. "I don't need foreplay. Just love me, Holt." He barked a throaty, purely masculine laugh.

Pushing away from her, he raised her hips to his, adjusting their bodies so that they were in perfect alignment. "Your wish—" he stopped, slowly pressing into her body "—is my—" he fed her another inch of himself "—command." He pressed home.

"Ohhhhh." Yasmine released her pent-up breath in one long whoosh of air as he gave her all of himself.

Her chest moved up and down harshly, and her tongue came out to wet her dry lips.

The room was in shadows, the only light coming from the kitchen. In the dim light, she saw his bright blue eyes clearly as he stared down at her. She felt the muscles in his forearms tremble slightly when she placed her hands on them, her nails scoring into his skin at the feel of his thickness invading her body.

It had been several weeks since they'd last made love, and she felt her walls contract and release on his shaft.

She held her body still, his thickness seeming to take up every bit of space inside her.

He closed his eyes, and sank his face into the curve of her neck. "Baby…" he groaned.

The steady tightening and releasing of her walls around his shaft made him grit his teeth, the strain of holding back and not just pushing into her silken warmth torturous.

Yet he didn't move, waiting for her. For Yasmine, he'd wait an eternity if he had to.

"Are you okay?" he asked, and she nodded her head.

"I'm okay," she panted, but still he waited, wanting to make sure she was ready for him. He licked his finger and ran it over her clit, moistening it even more as he slowly massaged the straining nub.

"Holt," she moaned, dragging his name out as he pinched and massaged the tightening nub.

As impatient as he was to rock inside her tight, warm sheath, he wanted it to be good for her, as well.

He wanted to devour her, saturate himself in her essence and make love to her in ways that would force her to realize how much he cared about her.

How much he loved her.

The dawning realization that he loved her had hit him the moment he saw Clayton Moore kissing her.

It was at that moment, even as he knew she hadn't been returning his kiss, overhearing the conversation and the deep-seated knowledge that she would never betray him like that, he'd felt a paralyzing fear.

Fear that she'd come to mean so much to him, and that she'd someday leave him.

He glanced down at her through a haze of love and lust at the same time as she wrapped her legs around his lean hips, anchoring her feet against the middle of his back, and arched into his embrace.

"God, Yasmine, I missed you," he said roughly against her throat as he slowly began to glide inside her. He pulled away so that he could see her face as he made love to her.

He had to see her face. Had to let her see *him,* as he made love to her.

"I missed you, too, Holt," she whispered back as he carefully rocked into her.

Slowly he made love to her. Took his time with her, placing careful kisses over her face, down her throat, before capturing one of her breasts within his mouth. He sucked hard on the distended nipple, making her cry out and arch her body up, meeting his downward stroke.

When she repeated the move, pushing her body upward just as he stroked down, he could no longer hold back. Grabbing her hips, he picked up the pace, his strokes becoming faster, more demanding.

"Holt, Holt…oh, oh, oh, ohhhhhh." Her moaning litany became frantic cries as he felt her body trembling violently against his. "Baby…baby, I'm com—" she screamed, her mewling cries bouncing off the walls and reverberating around the room. He felt her hands on his back, scoring deeply, yet he continued to shift and thrust inside her body, not ready to give in to the release he felt ready to consume them both.

"I love you, Holt!" he heard her cry from a distance, behind the roaring in his ears.

"God, I love you!" He grasped her hips tightly, his fingers digging into the fleshy skin of her hips, and thrust deeply inside her. After one more, deep stroke, her walls clamped down on him, and unable to hold back, he gave in to his release, and together they reached the pinnacle in unison.

"Do you love me enough to marry me?"

Holt felt Yasmine's body stiffen against him, the hands that had been feathering his arm that lay crosswise over her chest coming to a standstill.

She didn't say anything for such a long time, he wondered if she'd heard him.

"Did you hear me?"

"I did," she said softly. When she said nothing more, his heart fell to his gut.

"You may as well say yes, Yas," he said softly.

Caught off guard, she turned to face him. "Oh, yeah? And why is that?"

"I told everybody that when I came back, I would be bringing my bride with me."

"And what's going to happen if you don't?" she asked. Although it was dark and he could barely make out her features, Holt detected a lightness in her response, one that eased the tension, making him relax against her.

"Hmm….maybe your aunt's reaction when you tell her you're pregnant?" he said, running a hand over her flat stomach, reminding her that they hadn't used a condom.

From the sound of his voice, it didn't seem as though he minded if she were pregnant.

She paused and glanced up at him. "I think we have a few things to talk about before we discuss you being my baby daddy…don't you?" Yasmine quipped back, forcing a lightness to her voice she wasn't feeling.

He wanted to marry her.

She was just getting over the fact that he'd come after her and that he loved her.

He sighed, again moving her so that her bottom was snug against his shaft.

"Yes, I guess we do."

"Why do you do that?"

"What?" he asked, nuzzling the back of her head.

"Whenever we talk you move me so I can't see

your face. You did the same thing when we were in Sheridan."

She felt his shrug. "It's easier for me that way, I guess."

She digested that while she waited for him to speak. "Yas, I owe you, you know."

She frowned. "What for?"

"For forcing me to see who I was, who I'd allowed everyone to think I was." He stopped. "By opening up to me, and not expecting anything in return."

Yasmine closed her eyes, remembering how hard it had been not to shake him and make him open up to her. How hurt she'd felt after opening up to him, letting all her emotions show, and him not giving her anything back. How hurt she'd felt when he closed her out. The memory of what it felt like when she thought she meant nothing to him.

"You made me see myself, forced me to look at myself in ways that were damned uncomfortable," he said, his voice low.

They were silent after that, each lost in their own thoughts, before Holt spoke.

"Everything isn't a joke to me, Yas," he said, reminding her of what she'd said to him in Sheridan. "It's just that I've operated under the same M.O. for so long, hiding my feelings, keeping it all locked down, it became who I was. Someone afraid," he said, the admission torn from him.

"Afraid of what?" she asked softly, her hand coming up to cover his.

He laughed, without humor. "Afraid to love, I guess. To get close enough to anyone to be that vulnerable." He shook his head. "Afraid that if I did, they'd leave, eventually."

"What about your father?" she asked. "Your brothers…Aunt Lilly. You love them."

She felt his shrug against her back. "That's a different kind of love. Family love. And they first showed me how to love. They showed me that I could trust someone enough to do that. That they wouldn't leave me. Like my…" He stopped.

His mother.

Yasmine knew of Holt's background from her aunt, knew that he'd come to the boys' home after getting into trouble constantly at school. When the social workers were finally called in it was to see he was living in a beat-up group home, basically raising himself. The house was in shambles, and there was no sign of his mother.

"My mother left me when I was barely old enough to take care of myself. But even before she physically left, she wasn't there mentally—half the time she was out at one of the local bars, the other half she was at home drunk. I got used to taking care of myself."

"Is that how you ended up in the boys' home?" she asked. Even though she already knew the answer, she wanted him to tell her. Wanted him to open up to her, wanted him to know that he could trust her, even with things that made him feel exposed.

"Yeah," he said, sighing heavily. "And things didn't

change for me much there. I was still raising hell," he said, and laughed lightly. "If Jed Wilde hadn't taken me in, I don't know where I would have been, what kind of man I would have turned into." He stopped.

"Where did she go?" she asked softly, after a moment. "Your mother?"

"I don't know. But it didn't matter. At least that's what I convinced myself, anyway. She said she was heading to California, but I've never heard from her since she dropped me off at the home. But that's all in the past. I'm a big boy now," he said.

"I'll say," she quipped, wiggling her butt against him, seeking to lighten his mood.

"Enough of that, woman, or we won't get to finish this 'talk' you seem hell-bent on us having."

Yasmine sobered. "I don't want you to think you have to tell me anything you don't want to. I—I don't want to bring up things that make you unhappy, Holt."

He turned her around to face him. "You haven't and you don't. I want to tell you. Because I love you."

Yasmine smiled, blinking away the tears she felt burning her eyes. After a long kiss, he released her.

"I—I decided to pass on Clayton's offer," she said after the kiss ended.

Holt's hands stilled on her back.

"About that….baby, I'm sorry. I totally made a jack-ass of myself and I'm sorry. Please don't pass up an opportunity like this because of me. You don't have to. We'll find a way—"

She placed a finger over his mouth and explained the

idea that had taken root while she'd been on the ranch, and the producers' immediate love for the idea.

He frowned.

"Did I have anything to do with that decision?"

She rolled her cheek against the finger running over her skin. "Maybe," she said, and he leaned down to capture her lips. Once he released her, the worried look returned to his face.

"What's this for?" she asked running her hand between his brows.

He captured her finger, pulling the small digit into his mouth, then slowly releasing it. "I was wrong to say what I did to you. You've got to know I've never regretted saying anything more than when I hurt you."

He watched her dark, soulful eyes stare into his, the look in them uncertain, as though she didn't fully believe what he was saying.

With a groan, he pulled her close, slanting his mouth over hers, kissing her with all the love he had for her, hoping that in action he could make up for what he'd done to her with his words. Finally, he released her.

Placing his palms over her face, he forced her to look at him. "And I promise you I will never give you a reason to doubt me, my love for you. And if you agree to marry me—" his words came to a stop, emotion clogging his deep voice "—I don't have the words, Yas. Just please marry me, love me…" He stopped, and Yasmine drew in a deep breath.

"You complete me, Yasmine. All I'm asking is that you let me prove to you that I'm worthy of your love.

The last weeks without you have been pure hell. And I don't want to live my life without you. I can't breathe without you," he finished in a voice so low, she barely picked up the words he said.

Along with the raw emotion she saw reflected in his light blue eyes, Yasmine saw love and honesty there, as well.

She loved this man with everything she had in her. Had loved him for as long as she could remember. The month she'd spent on the ranch had only sealed a fate that had been theirs all along.

Yasmine closed her eyes briefly. When she opened them, she reached for him and pulled him close, wrapping her arms tightly around him, tears slowly easing down her face.

He laughed, his voice husky, catching her before she tumbled them off the sofa. "I guess this means yes?" he asked, but despite the laugh, she heard his voice tremble. She bobbed her head up and down, unable to speak past the constriction in her throat.

With a loud "whoop!" of joy he tightened his hold on her, pulling away from her far enough to see her face.

"It's about time you made an honest man of me... What took you so long?" he asked, and tugged her back down, slanting his mouth over hers, swallowing her startled laughter.

* * * * *

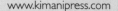

REQUEST YOUR FREE BOOKS!

2 FREE NOVELS
PLUS 2 FREE GIFTS!

KIMANI™
ROMANCE

Love's ultimate destination!

KROM11

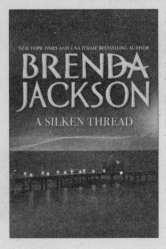